A
Midwinter's
Tail

A
Midwinter's
Tail

LILI HAYWARD

SPHERE

SPHERE

First published in Great Britain in 2023 by Sphere

1 3 5 7 9 10 8 6 4 2

A CIP catalogue record for this book
is available from the British Library.

Hardback ISBN 978-1-4087-2955-7

Typeset in Garamond by M Rules
Printed and bound in Great Britain by
Clays Ltd, Elcograf S.p.A.

Papers used by Sphere are from well-managed forests
and other responsible sources.

Sphere
An imprint of
Little, Brown Book Group
Carmelite House
50 Victoria Embankment
London EC4Y 0DZ

An Hachette UK Company
www.hachette.co.uk

www.littlebrown.co.uk

For my parents

So in peace our tasks we ply,
Pangur Bán, my cat, and I;
In our arts we find our bliss,
I have mine and he has his.

Practice every day has made
Pangur perfect in his trade;
I get wisdom day and night
Turning darkness into light.

'PANGUR BÁN', ANONYMOUS,
TRANSLATED BY ROBIN FLOWER

PROLOGUE

Morgelyn

D id I ever tell you the story of this island, Mina, and how it got its name?

You see, once upon a time it wasn't an island at all, but part of a beautiful land called Lyonesse; a fair and shining place of fields and great stone roads, houses and vineyards where people grew rich on the bright tin pulled from the ground, and merchants from across the world came to barter and live in ease.

Until one dark Midwinter's Eve, when the people of Lyonesse were so caught up in their merrymaking, in their spices and tin and riches, that they forgot to give thanks to the sea. And the sea, having always calmed its waves for them, was angry at being forgotten. More than angry, it was furious, roaring with rage as only the sea can.

Of course, the people of Lyonesse realised their folly at once, but it was too late. In desperation they flung gold into the waves, but the sea dashed it all to pieces against the rocks, where it turned to bright gorse. They poured gallons of their finest wines into the raging surf, but the sea spat it back in a shower of spray, where the droplets turned to purple heather. Finally, they cast the bright tin that had made them rich into the depths, only for the sea to scatter it into moonlight.

And the water began to rise, higher than the thresholds, then higher than the windows and finally higher than the tallest church tower. The waves crashed down like a hundred hammers on a thousand anvils, and that fine land and its entire people were lost.

All save one girl, named Morgelyn.

She was as gentle as the dawn and as poor as a ship's mouse, and she lived, not in a grand palace, but in a tumbledown cottage on the beach with her faithful cat, Murr. And though she had no gold or jewels, she alone remembered to honour the sea, with a humble little wreath made from sea holly and heather. So when the sea roared its wrath and the waters swallowed the cottage, Murr used secret magic to turn that wreath into a raft, where she and Morgelyn hung on for dear life.

And as Lyonesse drowned, girl and cat were tossed upon the waves, until finally they came to rest, soaked and frozen, upon a rocky mountain top.

'Oh Murr, a poor Yuletide we'll have,' Morgelyn cried, 'with nothing but salt for our meal and rocks for our bed!'

If the sea was angry, Murr was doubly so.

Since there is nothing like the electric fury of a cat to catch attention, the sea looked up at the mountain top, and saw the girl and her cat and the humble wreath they had made in its honour, and felt ashamed.

And as quickly as the sea's temper had risen, it fell, but the deed was done. The glittering land of Lyonesse was lost, and all that remained were the tops of the tallest mountains, including the one where Morgelyn sat, holding Murr and shivering.

So the sea gathered up kelp and brought it to the shore as a blanket. It found branches of sweet gorse and fragrant heather, caught limpets and mussels, clams and oysters and scattered them across the rock like jewels so the girl and the cat could eat. It found driftwood from the four corners of the globe and brought it to them, so they might build themselves a shelter.

And in time, the waters fell and the mountain tops became islands and, well, you know the rest, dear Mina.

Of course, if you ask people about this story they will laugh and say that I'm a foolish old man. But that's because the words were never written down, or if they were, they've long turned to sea foam. I only know it because Murr told me, and she should know, because that rock where Morgelyn found shelter? It was this very island. And the driftwood hut they built? That was this cottage. And the cat who saved her from the storm?

Why, that was none other than Murr herself.

CHAPTER ONE

The call of a curlew fills my ears, haunting above the tiny, secluded cove. In the winter twilight, the waves are gentle, soft as velvet covering a fiercely beating heart.

The sign has been scoured by the weather, lost beneath lichen, but I know what it says. The letters are traced in salt spray on my lips.

Morgelyn.

When last I walked here, the heather on the headland towered above me and there was a hand holding mine, guiding my steps. Now, I'm alone. Taking a breath I make my way down towards the shore, into the maze of furze.

A rustle, a snap and the hairs on my neck rise with the feeling of being watched. In the shadows beneath the winter-blooming gorse, sea-green eyes blink into being.

'Murr?'

I take a step forwards, only for the cat to turn tail and disappear in a flurry of grey paws.

'Murr!'

I race down the narrow path, following the cat who always remains a few steps beyond my reach, leading me this way and that through the wild gorse until, at last, the soil beneath my feet turns to sand, and I find myself standing on the shore. Up ahead, a cottage glows in the twilight, a ship's lantern hanging from an old hook, illuminating grey stone and a weather-beaten door, where someone sits, waiting . . .

'Mina?'

I look up with a jolt. No curlew's cry, just the distant wail of a siren echoing from the streets below. London's lights resolve themselves through the polished window, reflected in the dark waters of the Thames.

'You OK?' Paola asks, handing me another glass of champagne.

'Yes, sorry.' I pull a smile onto my face. 'Miles away.'

Years.

All around, our company's Christmas party is in full swing. The private penthouse bar is a wonderland of plastic fir trees twinkling with fairy lights, fake snowdrifts scattered across the floor and huge, reflective baubles that distort people's faces like fun mirrors at a carnival. Novelty ties are gradually loosening millimetre by millimetre, cheeks growing shiny as the glasses of champagne circulate, knocked back on stomachs empty but for tiny, tasteful canapés – a disc of turkey meat, a sphere of cranberry gel – served by waiting staff dressed in fashionable Nordic knitted jumpers and Santa hats. I take another hefty sip of champagne. It's still only 16 December; Christmas seems to start earlier every year.

'Any sign of our target?' I ask, trying to remember what I was meant to be doing.

Paola's glittery nails drum a pattern on her phone as she nods towards the bar.

'Ten o'clock.'

There he is, in an impeccable blue suit, drinking whisky rather than the free champagne, a flash of tartan sock at the ankle his only concession to the season. Jeremy Hunter-Thorpe is the client on every agency's Christmas wish list, the one who might save me from being fired, *if* I can snag him for our company before the year is out.

'I can't believe he's here,' Paola whispers. 'It's fate. Have you spoken to him yet?'

I shake my head, champagne fizzing in my nose. 'It's not exactly fate when this is the closest members' bar to his office.'

'Come *on*, Mina. You know him, don't you?'

'My dad does.' I wince. 'They play golf.'

Paola gives me a wry smile. She's our team's assistant and one of the only friends I have at work. She's also too kind to bring it up, but we both know what people whisper about me around the coffee machine: *Only got the job because her father knows half the city. Why else would Marianne hire her? She's useless.*

It isn't true, but I can't really blame them for thinking it. Most of them are so ambitious it makes my head spin, even without the mutters from management about 'downsizing' the team ... *Work lacks conviction* – that was the feedback from my last appraisal. No matter how many proposals I put forward, or designs I work on, or times I tell myself I'm lucky to have this job, it still feels like I'm trying to wear a version of myself that doesn't quite fit. I know it, and I know *they* know it.

With a deep breath, I square my shoulders. Dad's connections or not, if I bring in Hunter-Thorpe they'll *have* to think twice about keeping me on. Defiantly, I down the rest of the champagne – too fast. It splashes my chin, dripping onto the expensive green silk dress I borrowed from my stepmother Julia in an attempt to be 'festive'.

'Shit!'

Paola's ready as ever, stepping in front of me. 'Go and clean up,' she says. 'I'll keep an eye on him.'

'Right, thanks.'

At a half-run, I grab my handbag from the concierge and escape to the ladies. It's empty, thankfully, choir-sung carols piped in from somewhere, masking the chatter of the party.

I saw three ships come sailing in, on Christmas Day, on Christmas Day . . .

Mid-December and it still feels a thousand years until Christmas is over and done with. Two more weeks of worn-out songs on the radio and adverts for parties in every bar and eggnog-flavoured coffee and *where will you be spending the holidays, Mina?* I lean on the tinsel-decorated sink, missing my mum with the sort of sudden, sharp pang that still takes me by surprise, even after all these years. Without her, Christmas has always felt . . . empty. Nothing more than a day of awkward small talk with my father and stepmother, all the while trying not to remember how magical it once felt. Sighing, I blot at the champagne with a paper towel, then dig around in my bag for the lipstick I flung in there earlier.

Of course, it's nowhere to be found. I pull out handfuls of junk: tissues, old lip balms, ink drawing pens that I haven't used for months but can't bear to throw away, a crumpled envelope . . .

Frowning, I turn the envelope over. It's the size of my hand and very scruffy, the original address pasted over with a floral sticker, presumably forwarded from my father's address by Julia. I dimly remember scooping it up from the mailbox in a rush the previous morning, before yet another fourteen-hour workday put it out of my mind.

I flip it over. There's a return address in spidery green ink.

Morgelyn, Isles of Scilly, Cornwall.

My heart gives a triple beat, and for an instant, beneath the carols, I think I hear the call of a sea bird.

Part of me wants to throw the envelope in the bin or shove it back into my bag unread, but my fingers betray me, working at the paper to tear it open.

Immediately, a scent wafts out, battling with the festive spice air freshener: a combination of crushed greenery and a whiff of turpentine, so familiar that it hurts. In a daze, I stick my hand into the envelope, only to prick myself on something sharp and drop the whole thing, spilling the contents onto the tiles.

Blood wells in a single bead on my finger. I lick it off and taste iron, staring at the impossible object that lies on the floor: a key, made from rusted metal, a hundred years old if it's a day. A slip of paper is tightly wrapped around its length like a ribbon, holding a sprig of a strange, spiky, ghostly green plant.

Sea holly. The name comes to me as if someone whispered it in my ear.

Morgelyn.

Hesitantly, I pick up the key. It's heavy in my palm, like something from a story, real and half-imagined at the same time. The paper comes away with a gentle hush, and I unwind it to read the message, written in green ink in a hand I never thought I'd see again:

Mina – please look after her

'Davy?' I whisper.

The bathroom door creaks, letting in a blast of party noise and someone singing about how they wished it could be Christmas every day.

'What's taking so long?' Paola hisses. 'He looks like he's about to leave!'

'Just coming,' I call dazedly, still staring at the key. Why is it here in a London bathroom and not in the pocket of yellow oil-skin jacket, wet with sea spray? Why is it not hanging on a hook, beside a blue, weather-beaten door that opens onto a sandy path?

Light paws, bounding over rocks towards me. Eyes bright as gorse flowers. Hot chocolate in my numbed hand, sweetness mingling with the salt on my lips. My mother's laugh as we dashed from the waves. A man's soft voice, weaving a Christmas Eve ghost story as a storm lashed the windows.

'Hey!' Paola snaps her fingers. 'Earth to Mina.'

I'm back in the bathroom, and outside the party lurches on, waiting for me to smile and nod.

'Yes, coming.' Hurriedly, I shove the key and the envelope back into my bag, run a hand through my mouse-brown curls to check they haven't gone frizzy, and follow Paola into the party.

'Go on,' she mutters, looping a string of gold tinsel around my neck like a scarf, 'you can do it.'

I'm not so sure I can. My head is swimming with questions about the key and the strange note, but I raise my chin and walk up to the man at the bar.

'Mr Hunter-Thorpe?' I ask, trying to sound confident. 'I'm Mina Kestle. I think we might have met once or twice before?'

'Kestle . . .' The man's eyes pass over the top of my head, looking for someone more important. 'Any relation to Jonathan Kestle?'

I give my best businesslike smile. 'My father.'

'*No!*' Hunter-Thorpe actually looks at me, his pouchy cheeks lifting in a smile as he takes in the tinsel. 'Oh, but of course, *Mina*. Didn't recognise you, you're all grown up.'

I help myself to another glass of champagne. 'That's right. I'm working nearby, as a marketing executive at Felder, Price and—'

'Yes, your father said you were doing something here. Didn't quite believe him. After all the fuss you put him through about being an artist.' He beams down at me indulgently. 'Gerard and I used to love your little Christmas cards.'

My smile grows strained. The cards were Dad's idea of playing office politics, getting me to draw special festive pictures for his clients and bosses every year. *The cute factor*, he always said. I didn't mind. It filled some of the time I was home from boarding school, and gave Dad and I something to talk to each other about. That was before art became a problem between us; a constant argument about wasted time and money that had finally exploded when he found out I'd applied for art school without his knowledge, rather than for a law degree, like he'd wanted me to.

I'm not going to fund you throwing your life away, he'd raged.

I'd left home that night, aged eighteen, and hadn't taken a penny of his money since. Was using his name to lure Hunter-Thorpe any different? I shove the thoughts aside.

'Well, I'm still involved in the creative side of things,' I say. 'Which is why I wanted to ask about your latest campaign. I had some thoughts about it, and was wondering if we could arrange a meeting?'

He eyes a tray of deconstructed mince pie cubes as it passes. 'I'm jam-packed until Christmas, but my secretary might be able to squeeze in a hot choc for old times' sake. We're going to Scotland for the holidays, Gerard and I and the kids. Excellent golf. You're spending it with your father?'

Did he just agree to a meeting? He's finishing the last of his whisky, as if about to leave. 'Oh, we don't really make a fuss about Christmas,' I murmur. 'But I'll make the appointment, so I can show you some ideas?'

'Fine, fine. First thing Wednesday. But on one condition.' He points his empty glass at me. 'That you'll send us another *charming* card. Gerry did so enjoy them.'

'Of course,' I say, trying to ignore the rush of embarrassment and frustration. 'I'd be happy to.'

'And say hello to your father!' he bellows, making his way towards the doors.

'Well?' Paola whispers, sidling over to me. Across the room, our boss Marianne is staring, her steely gaze at odds with the flashing reindeer antlers perched on her head.

'He agreed,' I say, slightly bewildered. 'He agreed to meet me before he leaves for the holidays, Wednesday morning . . .'

Paola puts her glass down with a clink, adjusting her own tinsel scarf. 'I'm telling Marianne.'

I watch as she hustles away towards our boss. All at once the party is too much, the music and the chatter painfully loud. Grabbing my drink, I escape onto one of the balconies. They've made an effort out here too, with faux-fur blankets on the seats, artificial fir branches and glittery plastic icicles decorating the railings. I catch a whiff of someone's cigarette smoke and sigh into the cold city air, my breath hanging before me like unformed words. I did it, scored a meeting with Hunter-Thorpe, just like everyone wanted. So why do I feel so empty?

Reaching into my bag, I pull out the key. A horrible, leaden thought has been forming, ever since I saw it. And those words: *Please look after her.*

Who – *what* – could he mean? And why would it have anything to do with me, unless . . .?

'There you are.' Paola rushes out of the party, cheeks glowing. 'Marianne's *face* when I told her – I thought she'd swallowed the olive in her Martini.' When I nod vaguely in response, her smile falters. 'Mina, what is it? And what's that?'

'I think it's the key to my godfather's cottage,' I hear myself say, as if the idea isn't absurd.

'You have a godfather?'

'Had. Haven't spoken to him since I was a kid.' I hand over the key, the coiled note.

Paola frowns at it. '"Her." Who's he talking about?'

Fur clung with cold, smelling of the wild sea, a warm, heavy weight at my side, singing me to sleep as a storm howled outside the window.

I shake my head to clear away the memory. 'I'm not sure. Davy used to have a cat, called Murr, but that was years ago.'

She squints at the note. 'So he's asking you to look after his cat? Is he going away for Christmas or something?'

The knot of worry in my stomach tightens at those words. As far as I remember, Davy rarely left the islands, rarely left his cottage and his beach. I pull out my phone and, as Paola asks whether I'm OK, type the name I've pushed away for almost two decades.

Davy Penhallow

I click on the top entry. It takes me to a web page called *Artists of Cornwall*.

Davy Penhallow
Seascape painter of Morgelyn, Isles of Scilly
A famously reclusive writer, artist and poet, known as the 'Old Man of the Sea' for his exceptional winter seascapes. Penhallow's works reflect a deep knowledge of Cornish folklore, myth and legend, and a love for his home on the tiny storm-tossed island of Morgelyn, 28 miles south-west of the tip of Cornwall.

There's a thumbnail; a decades-old black and white photo showing him just as I remember. Rumpled fair hair streaked with grey, shy smile, wearing a knitted fisherman's jumper. He's holding a cat in his arms; a huge, grey, furry creature almost blurred out by the photograph.

But there are no contact details beyond the address of a gallery on St Martin's, one of the larger islands.

Paola asks again, but I can't answer. That picture of Davy has brought a memory flooding back, as indistinct as the badly rendered photograph. A magical Christmas from so many years ago; my last truly happy Christmas, in fact. I remember a boat ride on the wild seas, an open hearth, a tiny shop, the feel of my mother's soft jumper against my cheek as people sang late into the night inside an old village pub. I remember twinkling, painted decorations, the salt-green smell of sea holly, a story of other worlds spun by the hearth on Christmas night.

The cold, smoky air stings my eyes, and I realise they are wet with tears.

'Mina,' Paola takes my arm. 'What is it?'

I swipe at my face, forgetting about my make-up. 'Sorry. It's just a shock. We haven't spoken for nearly twenty years. And now this.' I look at the key again. 'What the hell am I supposed to do?'

She raises a perfectly sculpted brow. 'Can't you call him to ask?'

'He doesn't have a phone. Or if he does, I don't have the number.' I half-close my eyes, thinking. It's all so long ago. But wasn't there a phone box on the island, corroded by the salt, its red paint worn pink by the winds? 'Wait . . .'

I tap in a new search on my phone, and after a bit of scrolling, I find a listing on what looks like a telephone box enthusiast's website.

Telephone Box. Outside the Helm Inn.
Morgelyn. Cornwall.

There's a number listed. I hit dial, knowing it's probably ridiculous; that it was probably disconnected years ago. But after a long silence, it starts to ring. Paola makes a *now what* face at me as I stand, phone pressed to my head, with London's traffic rushing by floors below, trying to imagine a windswept island hundreds of miles away, a telephone box ringing and ringing into the night, lonely as a lost ship's bell.

I'm just about to give up, when there's a click.

'Hello?' a distant voice answers, like a ghost.

My voice sticks in my throat. What on earth do I say?

'Hello,' I repeat.

'Who's this?'

The line's bad, crackling and fuzzing. Is that the sea I can hear in the background, crashing against the shore? 'This is Mina,' I blurt. 'Um, Mina Kestle. I'm just calling to . . . I'm wondering if . . . do you know someone called Davy Penhallow? He lives there, on Morgelyn. I think.'

My cheeks blaze, despite the frosty air of the balcony. They only grow warmer when a long silence stretches on the other end of the phone, filled with that strange, rushing roar that might be waves or might be the sound of hundreds of miles, of my call racing across a network to reach a far-flung receiver.

'Hello? Are you still there?'

'What did you say your name was?' The voice has a strong Cornish ring to it, all rounded vowels and burrs that do nothing to hide the sharpness of suspicion.

'I . . . my name's Mina Kestle. I was, I guess I still *am*, Davy's goddaughter.' The silence on the other end grows thicker. 'I got a strange letter from him, you see. And I just wondered if he's . . . if he's all right?'

'He's alive if that's what you mean. In hospital on St Mary's.'

My hand goes to my mouth. Beside me, Paola is making frantic *what's going on, what's he saying* faces. I wave for her to wait. 'What happened?'

'Jem found him a week ago, collapsed on the path. Might've lain there for hours if it hadn't been for old Murr. Yowling her head off, she was, till someone heard and came looking.'

'My God. Is he OK?'

There's a long silence, filled with twenty years of the unsaid. 'No, Miss Kestle. I'm afraid he isn't.'

Did I ever tell you, Mina, the story of the girl who thought she had lost everything?

It was Midwinter's Eve. A night for old words, the hinge of the year when the doors between worlds stand open and anything that has been might be again, and anything that will be hangs in the balance.

The girl should not have strayed abroad on such a night, not on Yule, when all were bright and merry and throats were warm with wine and spices. But the girl felt no joy, only sorrow, for she had lost the one she loved. And so, in the deepest part of that longest night, she stood upon the shore and wished she could be with him once again.

A dangerous wish on such an eve. The piskies heard her and told the spriggans, and the spriggans hissed the news to the buccas – the sea spirits who make mischief beneath the waves. And they came creeping out of the sea on feet made from foam, with their shining fishes' eyes and their hair as green and clinging as weeds.

'Why not join us?' they sang. 'Your love waits beneath the waves.'

And the girl stepped into the icy surf up to her ankles. It bit at her skin, soaked through her heavy stockings, and the buccas crooned all the louder.

'We have been waiting for you long, so long. Why not come to him? Why linger on the shore?'

And the girl stepped into the waves up to her knees, her skirt billowing out like a drowning sail, and the buccas sang louder still.

'Come down to our lost halls. Come celebrate Yule with sunken gold and the songs of drowned sailors. There is nothing for you on land.'

And just as she was about to step up to her neck, she heard a noise beneath the wind, a loud cry that made her turn back. There on the shore stood a large cat, with fur as grey as smoke and eyes as green as glass.

The cat hissed at the buccas, sparks flying from her coat, green eyes flaring, and the buccas wailed in frustration that their prize might be snatched from them.

The cat growled and the buccas sank beneath the waves until only their sad fishes' eyes showed.

The cat spat and swiped at the frothing foam with her paw, and sent them fleeing back to their drowned halls, empty handed.

And the girl realised that there was nothing beneath the waves for her after all. She turned and waded back towards the shore, to where the cat waited, proud and solemn in the moonlight.

'Thank you,' she told the cat, shuddering in her sodden clothes.

The cat simply raised her tail. Follow me, that gesture said.

She did, and by and by she saw a cottage, glowing like a jewel in the night, every window lit with candles and lanterns, the scent of warm spices and hot roasting meat and freshly baked bread spiralling out into the darkness.

The cat yowled at the door to be let in and as soon as the people in the cottage saw the girl, they bundled her inside, wrapped her in thick blankets, gave her cider spiked with saffron and cloves and brandy to drink, and set her before the hearth, where the cat leaped into her lap, to banish the sea's chill from her bones.

And as she fell asleep, the cat began to purr; a sound that was like a song, older than words, older than time. A song of leaf and shoot, *of the sun on the waves and the songbird returning, the drone of bees among the heather and the quiet creak of a buried seed, stretching towards the light. A song of life. A song of hope.*

The girl slept, and the grey cat settled down to wash and watch as Midwinter's Eve slipped into Midwinter's Day.

CHAPTER TWO

I hurry up the stairs from the Tube into Paddington Station. Even though it's gone eleven, the concourse is busy, Christmas shoppers laden with purchases from chaotic Oxford Street, students slung with tote bags heading home for the holidays, hooting gaggles of office workers staggering back from dinners and parties, their voices ringing from the iron and glass roof. The girders have been decorated, wound around with plastic holly garlands and vast red and gold baubles that spiral and catch the light. I dodge a dancing businessman dressed in a snowman costume and pull out my phone.

'All right,' Paola says briskly. In the background, I can hear the office party still going strong. 'There's one last train this evening, but you have to hurry because it's leaving in five minutes. Platform one.'

My heels clack on the tiled floor as I race towards the edge of the station. 'What time does it get in?'

'Seven a.m. It's the sleeper.' I hear her sigh. 'Mina, are you *sure* you're OK? I still think you should wait until tomorrow.'

But some instinct pushes on, one that whispers *tomorrow might be too late.*

'I'm fine, I promise.'

'If you're sure.' She sounds doubtful.

My thoughts fly at a hundred miles an hour as I spot the train on platform one. 'I'll need to get to the islands from . . . where's the end of the line? Penzance?'

'I looked into that while you were on the Tube. There was only one option so I reserved it for you. I'm forwarding you the details now.'

'You're a star. I'll call you later. Thanks again!'

I sprint the last few steps towards the train, where the conductor already has a whistle in her mouth. She gestures me on and I *just* make it, leaping on board as the doors bleep and clatter shut behind me. Chest heaving, I brace myself against the wall of the corridor. It isn't until the brakes release and Paddington slides away like smudged paint outside the window that the reality of what I'm doing hits me.

What *am* I doing? Jumping onto a sleeper train after a single phone call? Paola's right, I should have gone home, sat down and planned this sensibly, not made a snap, drunken decision for a man who's almost a stranger. And yet . . . I remember how serious the man on the phone sounded as he explained that Davy had not yet regained consciousness; how worried they all were for him.

But you don't know him, a sour part of me insists. *He doesn't mean anything to you any more.*

I pull out my phone to check where the train next stops, to reconsider, when the ticket inspector steps through the doors. He looks cheerful, tinsel wound around his official cap.

'Good evening, miss,' he greets. 'Ever travelled with us on the Night Riviera before?'

'Yes,' I tell him. 'But it was years ago. And I, err, need a ticket.'

I'm half hoping he'll scowl and turf me off the train for not having a reservation, but instead he grins at my party attire. 'Last minute jaunt, eh? You're in luck, we've a few cabins free.'

I have to suppress a small scream when he tells me the price of the ticket, but it's too late now. Before I know what's happening, I'm stepping through the door of a tiny cabin. There, despite all the nerves and confusion, I feel a thrill of excitement at the sight of the bunk bed with its crisp sheet and tartan blanket, the sink, the reading lamp with its prim ribbon decoration, and outside, a dark city passing in a blur of light. I touch my hand to the cold glass, just as I did as an eight-year-old.

'Why hasn't Davy come to us for Christmas before, Mummy?'

'He doesn't like the city, sweetheart. And he has his cat to look after.'

'A cat?'

'Yes, a grey cat called Murr.'

'Murr's a funny name.'

'You'll have to ask Davy what it means. Now, go to sleep, there's a good girl. And when you wake up, we'll be by the sea.'

I swipe at my eyes and take out the note. In the dim lamplight, the writing is spidery and shaky, as if the hand that wrote it could barely hold a pen.

Mina – please look after her.

'Why, Davy?' I whisper.

Five words. Twenty years of silence and now just five words. No best wishes, no questions, no apologies. Just a request to look after a cat on an island so far from London it might as well be the end of the earth. When did he send it? I wonder, tracing those painstaking letters. And why to *me*? Did he know he was ill? If so, why didn't he write, call, anything?

I lie back on the swaying bunk and cover my eyes, as if that might block out the questions.

He's a selfish man, Mina. That's what my dad has always said about Davy. I thought he was just bitter because Mum wanted to move with me to the islands, after everything fell apart. But perhaps he's right. Perhaps, despite what the stranger on the phone said, none of this is my problem.

I'll visit the hospital, return the key, make sure the cat is looked after, and my responsibility will be done. I have my own life, my own problems, none of which Davy Penhallow ever gave a damn about.

The train rolls onwards, clacking through night-silent stations, and soon my eyes grow heavy, brain swimming with fading champagne and distant memories. They wash into my mind in fragments, like a beach full of broken shells. And if I pick one up, if I hold it to my ear, what will I hear?

Words, murmured on a stormy December night, as the wind howled and the waves crashed and the rain pattered against the windows.

Did I ever tell you, Mina, about this island?
Did I ever tell you . . .?

I wake, jolted from dreams of saltwater and song.

For a long moment I lie still, bewildered by the grey-carpeted ceiling and the stiff pillow beneath my head.

Then, I remember: Davy, the phone call, the train . . .

Scrambling up, I raise the blind and peer out. It's still dark, but false dawn is just beginning to paint the sky pink over the sleeping fields. Far away, a lone car's headlights beetle down a country lane.

A knock at the door sets off a pounding in my head. Staggering to my feet, I creak it open an inch. The conductor takes one look at my screwed-up face and grins. 'Just passed Truro, miss. Be getting into Penzance in about an hour. Will it be coffee, tea or our festive special, salted caramel hot chocolate?'

'Just tea, thanks,' I croak.

'Right you are.'

When I catch a glimpse of myself in the mirror, I realise I look about as bad as I feel, a hangover thudding into being, the whites of my eyes reddened in a way that just seems to emphasise the weird streak of grey in the brown of my left iris.

Where God changed his mind about the colour, Mum always said, her own bright brown eyes crinkled with laughter. I was teased at school about it, of course, and wished I had eyes of one colour like everyone else. It was only after she was gone that I was glad of it, because whenever I looked into the mirror and saw that grey fleck, I thought of her.

I wash off the smeared make-up as best as I can at the tiny sink and climb back beneath the blanket, huddling the cup of tea to my chest.

Outside, the sky grows lighter with every passing minute. Finally, the land on the other side of the track drops away and I see the sea. It shimmers just beyond the train line, pearlescent as the inside of a shell and so close I feel like I could leap into its icy grip.

St Michael's Mount, I remember my mother whispering, pointing to a dark hill in the distance, her hair tickling my face. *And beyond that, far out to sea, the islands. I think we'll be happy there, Mina . . .*

A tinny voice interrupts the memory. 'Good morning to all passengers. We will soon be arriving at Penzance, which is the end of the line. All change, please, and best wishes for the festive season.'

The moment I step onto the platform, sea air blasts my face, washing away the stuffy smell of the train. I breathe it deep, smelling brine and seaweed and wet sand.

Something within me stirs.

What's that poem that Mum always loved? The one she recited as we hurried down to the dock on that icy December morning, her cheeks pink with the cold wind and her eyes bright.

Exultation is the going of an inland soul to sea.

I dodge through the ticket hall, filled with yawning commuters and schoolchildren sloping in for the last week of distracted lessons, and make for the taxi rank, trying to find Paola's reservation. There was something in there about a transfer from Penzance station to the Isles, I'm sure of it . . .

As I look up, a coach pulls away to reveal a rather rickety-looking minibus, the words ISLES OF SCILLY TRAVEL painted across the side. A woman with an iron-grey bowl cut below a bright red bobble hat is staring straight at me. My face flushes as I hurry over.

'Morning,' I say awkwardly. 'Mina Kestle. I think I have a reservation?'

She looks at me closely, her blue eyes piercing as a gull's, before extracting a pencil from behind her ear. 'Kestle, Kestle . . . Yep, here you are. Hop on. You can pay at the terminal.'

As soon as I sag onto a musty bench seat, the woman climbs into the front.

'Is there no one else?' I ask.

'Not this time of year,' she yells as the radio bursts into life, a festive pop song blaring. 'Out of season.'

I try to relax as we drive through the town, try not to think about how rough the ferry crossing might be, until I notice we're driving *away* from the ferry terminal, not towards it. I lean forwards to shout to the driver.

'Excuse me, this *is* the transfer to the Isles of Scilly? To Morgelyn?'

'Sure is,' the woman yells back.

'Haven't we passed the ferry port?'

She lets out a hoot of laughter. 'Ferry doesn't run in December.'

'Then what . . .' We swing through a set of metal gates. Above them a weathered sign reads SCILLY AIR TRANSFERS. Horrified, I peer out of the window to see two tiny propeller planes waiting on a strip of runway.

'All change!' the woman calls, slamming on the brake so hard I nearly tumble from the seat.

A brisk breeze is blowing from the sea, making the wind socks above the airbase snap and flutter.

'Isn't there another way to get to the islands?' I ask the woman, staring at the tiny, toy-like planes.

'Nope,' she says, flinging the clipboard onto the front seat of the bus. As I stare, she pulls off the bobble hat and swaps it for a battered pilot's cap.

'You . . .' I look around, but the airstrip is deserted. 'Where's everyone else? Who's flying?'

'I am. Captain Lou Trevelyan at your service. And you're the only passenger.' She sniffs. 'Day looks a bit mizzley and there's a helm wind blowing, but we should be fine.' She pats at her pockets until she finds a hip flask, and takes a swig. 'Spot of brandy? Warm your cockles?'

The hangover curdles into horror. 'I think I'm going to be sick.'

'Paper bags are in the side pocket.' She claps her hands. 'Come on then, tide and time wait for no woman!'

CHAPTER THREE

For all my terror of taking to the sky in something that looks like a shoe with wings flown by a possibly inebriated pilot, the ride is vaguely thrilling. Everything feels unreal, as if I've peeled a version of myself away and left the other Mina back in London; the one who smiles and makes small talk about golf, the one who did the sensible thing and took the night bus home, the one who is even now waking up to the prospect of a weekend alone, searching for cheap train tickets to Cornwall with nothing but the washing up for company. Instead, I'm *this* Mina – the one who has spent more than she can afford to be the sole passenger of a tiny propeller plane, flying away from land and out across a ruffled grey sea.

'We'll land on St Mary's,' the pilot bellows. 'Tish'll meet you there.'

'Tish?' I yell back over the juddering and humming.

She flicks some controls. 'Tish – Leticia Strout, Davy's solicitor.' She glances at me over a pair of aviator sunglasses. 'That's why you're here, isn't it?'

My face burns. Of course she already knows who I am. The whole island probably does.

'Hold onto your hat,' she calls a few minutes later, 'we're coming in.'

Alarmed, I glance down. Through the clouds, I see islands, rocky outcrops of grey and heather-green, crescent moons of coves, gnawed by white-fanged waves. Another world, all that's left of a land lost beneath the sea. We start to drop so quickly that my stomach turns a somersault, and I see what looks like a handful of white buildings, a grass runway rising rapidly to meet us, or are we plummeting to meet it . . .?

The plane buzzes so low over the waves that I think we're not going to make it, and I grip the seat as we sink, bounce and the wheels skid on the slick grass before coming to a sudden halt.

The pilot looks around at me, hip flask in hand.

'*Yeghes-da!*' she beams.

I just about manage to grab the paper bag before I'm sick.

The airport is small, just a single-storey building with an information desk and waiting room, a plastic Christmas tree and a vending machine. In the toilets, I stare at my reflection, water dripping from my nose and now-frizzing hair. Why the hell *am* I here? I take a deep breath. Even a glimpse of the islands has brought memories swirling back into my mind like sand.

I wipe my face with paper towel, dig out a hair elastic and drag my hair back from my face.

Focus on the task in hand, I tell my tired-looking reflection. *Meet the solicitor, check on Davy in the hospital, hand over the key, ask about the cat, book a return flight, be back in London this evening. Simple.*

As I step out of the toilets, I hear voices coming from just out-side the airport doors. The pilot stands there, talking to a small woman with wild red hair and muddy boots, cheeks so pink she looks as if she's sprinted here.

'Oh, Lou,' a woman exclaims, 'you *didn't*.'

The pilot laughs. 'Couldn't help it.' There's the sound of a metal cap being unscrewed.

'Is that—?'

'Course not, it's just orange squash. You shoulda seen her face, though. Ruffazrats.'

'What would Davy say?'

I hear the pilot sniff. 'He'd think it was a laugh.'

'Well, it wasn't. That poor girl.'

'You won't be calling her that when she does what we think she's here to do. Jem says—'

'Jem should mind his mouth. We don't *know* what she's here to do, more's the point.'

As I shove open the door, she looks around. 'Miss Martinovszky!' she says, hurrying forwards. 'I'm Leticia Strout, I take care of your godfather's affairs.'

The name stops me in my tracks. No one has called me that in almost twenty years. Swallowing hard, I paste on the false smile I seem to wear more often than my real one these days. 'It's Kestle, actually. Martinovszky was my mother's name.'

The woman looks mortified. 'Oh, I'm so sorry. Davy always said ... well, that explains why we didn't find you sooner, of course.'

She still hasn't let go of my hand. If anything, she holds it tighter.

'I'm so sorry we're meeting like this. We would, of course, have contacted you, but ...' She trails off, already flushed cheeks turning crimson.

'Thank you,' I tell her, extracting my hand. 'And it's all right. It's no secret that Davy and I lost touch. It was why I was so surprised to receive the letter.'

'The letter, yes, the letter.' She seems flustered. 'Well, we can talk further at my office.'

The word *office* gives me pause. 'I was hoping to see Davy?'

'Of course. I'll take you there as soon as visiting hours start.'

'Thanks. Hopefully my stomach can manage a car.' I glance at the pilot.

She harrumphs and mutters something about the weather, before stomping away. Leticia watches her go. 'I'm sorry for Lou,' she says. 'She's good friends with Davy. I think all of this has shaken her more than she cares to admit.' She looks at me searchingly, as if to say, *And you?*

I keep my smile polite. 'Shall we go?'

The day brightens as we drive out of the airport in Leticia's beaten-up car, heading down the hill. A bay comes into view, pale sand and almost shockingly blue water, where boats bob gently. Despite the crisp December air, palm trees grow, some strung with fairy lights and glass fishing floats. Houses scatter the hillside, grey stone and whitewash, and beyond it all, the sea: a swathe of satin in the winter light. It's familiar, achingly so, like a half-remembered dream.

'Could you tell me about Davy?' I ask, as I sit stiffly in the seat. 'All I know is that he collapsed?'

Leticia nods sadly. 'Jem, one of Davy's neighbours, found him on the beach. As for what's wrong, we don't know for sure. A series of strokes, they think. They're giving him medication and so far he's stable. Not conscious, but stable.' She shakes her head. 'He's always been a private man, but in the last few months he's withdrawn almost completely. I think perhaps he'd been having episodes for some time and, like a proud old fool he . . .' Her voice cracks. 'Well, you know what he's like.'

Do I? My childhood memories of him exist as bright scraps; a kind old man with wild grey-streaked hair, the smell of turpentine and oil paint and ginger biscuits baking, the feel of sea-dried cotton beneath my cheek, a cat's constant purr. Memories which should be precious, but are soured by everything that came after: the long, cruel silence that felt like betrayal to my eight-year-old self. That *still* feels like betrayal.

I clear my throat. 'In his note Davy mentioned "her". Did he mean his cat?' Leticia doesn't answer straight away, navigating the tight, winding street between shops and buildings. 'He had one when I was little.'

She glances at me, an odd expression on her face. 'His cat. That's right.' Before I can ask more, she brings the car to a stop on a narrow side street. 'My office is just across the road.'

I follow her out onto what must be the main street of Hugh Town, the village that makes up the capital of the islands. It's busy on this bright Saturday morning, the windows of the shops merry with decorations, the onion-and-gravy smell from a Cornish pasty shop swirling tantalisingly into the air. Gulls wheel and cry, and above the rooftops I can see ships' masts down in the bay.

'Here we are,' Leticia announces outside a little bow-windowed shop, beneath a painted sign that declares:

STROUT & DAUGHTER
SOLICITORS

I can't help but smile a little. It's like something from a Dickens novel; the jolliest legal office I've ever seen. Fake snow clusters in the corners of the panes and an enormous wreath of sea holly and heather hangs from the door.

Inside, two desks dominate the space, stacks of files and folders everywhere. 'My daughter's not here today,' Leticia explains, switching on the lights and an ancient heater that smells like dust. 'Tea?'

I nod, if just to buy myself some time to think. Leticia seems happy to fuss and bustle about. For some reason, she seems more nervous than I am.

On one wall is an antique framed map showing the islands. I examine it, trying to knit together the flotsam of memories that remain from the few months I was here as a kid. St Mary's – where we are – is the 'big' island, then there's the long scatter of St Martin's, and Tresco, sandwiched next to wild Bryher, and to the south St Agnes and tiny Samson, and finally, the furthest out of all the islands, the last point of land before the vast deeps of the Atlantic, Morgelyn.

Something seems to whisper in my mind as I stare at it, and for a moment I think I smell apples, and winter greenery and snow . . .

'Here we are,' Leticia says, dumping a tray onto the desk, laden with milky teas and a huge plate of custard creams. I wrap my hands around the mug, and wait, as Leticia clears her throat.

'Thank you for coming here, Miss Kestle. This won't take long, I promise. Like I said, I am sorry we weren't able to reach you before, but we had no number and, seemingly, an old address.'

'It's all right. I understand.'

She nods uncomfortably. 'Miss Kestle, before I go on, might I ask, what are your expectations with regards to your godfather's estate?'

Estate. The word brings bad memories with it, of overheard conversations, papers, arguments, people with name badges asking me questions I didn't understand . . .

'I don't have expectations.' It comes out sharper than I intend. 'I'm just here to check on Davy, return the key.'

'Right, yes.' She takes a deep breath. 'The thing is, Miss Kestle, Davy had the foresight to name a guardian of his estate, in the event that he is incapacitated.' She hurriedly dunks a custard cream. 'It's you.'

'What do you mean, it's me?'

'You're the guardian.' She stuffs the biscuit into her mouth, as if that's the end of it.

'I don't understand.'

She chews for what seems like an age and takes a slurp of tea.

'Your godfather is an unusual man, Miss Kestle. He always has been. He left instructions that, in the event of his serious illness or death, control of his entire estate would be entailed upon –' she grabs another biscuit nervously '– the guardian of his cat, Murr.'

I stare at her. She can't be serious. This must be another joke, cooked up between the pilot and her to humiliate me. But she doesn't crack a smile. Instead, she chews intently, staring at me.

'Hold on. What does a cat have to do with this?'

'Well, the cat can't legally *inherit*, of course, but a guardian can be named to ensure the cat's continued safety and well-being. In the event of the cat's demise, ownership of the estate would pass to the guardian. And that's you.' She pulls a piece of paper from a perilously leaning stack and brandishes it at me. 'Sign here, please.'

I take the paper, staring down at the few short paragraphs of legalese, at the dotted space that awaits my name. 'What is it?'

'Just acknowledgement that I've told you Davy's wishes and that you accept the role of guardian.'

Despite the casualness of the words, there's a strange intensity in her expression as she hands over a ballpoint pen. I hear my dad's voice in my head as I look over the form.

Never sign anything without reading it.

I look it over as thoroughly as I can. The words themselves make sense, and spell out exactly what Leticia's told me. The situation, on the other hand ...

'Doesn't Davy have any family to do this?' I ask, hesitating.

A snort escapes Leticia as she munches on another biscuit. 'None he sees eye to eye with.'

'But ...' I look down at the legal wording, my head swimming. 'Why me?'

Leticia smiles. When she speaks, her voice is gentle. 'Davy told me once he felt that he had failed you as a godfather. He said he had promised your mother he would look out for you, and hadn't.' She shrugs a little. 'I think this was his way of trying to keep that promise.'

A coil of anger goes through me. Too little too late. I want to throw the paper back across the table. He turned his back when I needed him. And it's only now, when he needs *me*, that he makes a half-hearted attempt at reconciliation. Much as I hate to admit it, Dad was right. He is a selfish man.

But Leticia is watching me, and I can't help but see the sorrow in her expression, the concern. Davy means something to her, just as he once meant something to me. I pick up the tea and use it to wash down the emotion until I can speak without my voice shaking.

'Even if I sign, I don't know anything about looking after cats. I've never even had a hamster. And I'm going straight back to London.'

She nods understandingly. 'Of course.'

What harm could it do to agree? I think to myself. *It's what I came here to do, after all. And 'looking after' can just mean finding someone to care for the cat while Davy is ill. It's not the cat's fault its owner is self-centred.*

With a sigh, I lean down and scribble my name.

Leticia whisks the paper away. 'Thank you, Miss Kestle.' She smiles, as if in relief. 'Welcome to the islands.'

CHAPTER FOUR

My godfather lies motionless in the hospital bed, as silent as a statue, as if he's made from wood or stone rather than flesh, a figurehead worn by the sea and the wind, and laid down here, upon the starched sheets.

It's twenty years since I last saw him, waving goodbye from the docks, his face reddened by the cold sea breeze. I thought it would only be a week until I saw him again, never dreamed that when he turned his back it would be for years. Decades. Now, I stand in the doorway of the room, clutching at my handbag and feeling like a child masquerading as an adult. But the child I was is gone, and I am here, alone, staring at an old man I no longer know.

His hands rest on the sheets. When I was young, those hands seemed impossibly strong, breaking firewood and hauling rope, but now they are frail, the skin loose and crinkled, like brown paper used too many times. His hair – once a wild thatch of dark blond streaked with grey – is white as sea foam.

'Davy?' I murmur, and ridiculous hope rises in me that he'll stir and open those striking storm-grey eyes and smile his slow smile … But he doesn't. He only sleeps on, eyes flickering beneath the lids.

The key to his cottage hangs heavy in my pocket. What should I do with it now? I try to imagine him sealing it into the envelope, writing my name on the label and dropping it into a little island post box with what? Hope? Guilt?

'Well, it worked,' I tell him. 'I'm here.'

By the time I step from the hospital doors, having left my details with reception, a breeze has picked up, cool and fresh on my tired eyes.

'I assume you'd like to see the cottage?' Leticia asks as we walk down the hill towards Hugh Town, towards the impossible blue of the bay.

I check my phone. I do, and I don't. But there's still the cat to deal with and my return flight doesn't leave for nearly four hours. 'Do I have time?'

'Of course,' Leticia says, gently propelling me down the street, towards the harbour. 'It's only a short hop over to Morgelyn. The usual water taxis don't operate at this time of year, but someone should be able to run you across.'

For a moment I'm tempted to refuse, turn on my heel and hurry back towards the airport, signed paperwork or not. *Be an adult*, I tell myself. *Do what you've promised to do.*

We emerge onto a stone quayside, all storm-battered grey buildings and painted signs, fishing nets and sea floats and maritime paraphernalia everywhere. And beyond, the bay, glinting in the sunlight.

'I don't suppose you could take it?' I ask.

'Take what?'

'The cat.'

There's a horrified silence. '*Take* Murr?'

'Just while Davy's ill. Or maybe there's someone else on the island who could foster it?'

'No,' Leticia says firmly. 'Murr would never agree to leave the cottage.'

Agree?

Leticia's waving at someone up ahead. 'There's Gryff. You spoke with him yesterday. Gryff!'

A small boat bobs in the water, not much bigger than a dinghy. An old man stands in it holding a rope, dressed in a huge yellow oilskin jacket, a rainbow knitted hat crammed down over his head. I follow Leticia out onto the quayside, absurdly conscious of my high heels and handbag, my now-laddered tights, the thin, city mackintosh that does little to keep out the biting sea wind.

'This is Miss Kestle,' Leticia calls down. 'Davy's goddaughter. She'd like to go over to Morgelyn.'

The old man's eyebrows are thick and grey as mice. At the sight of me, they scurry beneath the brim of his knitted hat. 'She would, would she?'

I try for a smile, but mostly manage a grimace. 'Nice to meet you. Thank you for answering last night.'

He rubs his chin, as if embarrassed. 'Well. No luggage?'

'No, I'm just here for the day. I'm not staying.'

He glances at Leticia, then back at me, and shrugs. 'Best hop aboard then.'

I turn to the solicitor. 'I can call you, with any questions?'

'Of course. I'd come over with you, but the kids have their carol concert in a bit.' She hesitates, before pulling me into an abrupt hug. Her wild red hair tickles my face. 'Mina, he'd be so happy to know you're here.'

Before I can reply, she lets go and hurries off up the quay.

'Come on then,' Gryff calls up.

I make it down the rusted ladder and onto the boat in as dignified a manner as I can, half-tripping, half-collapsing onto the bench seat. It bobs violently, waves slopping its sides, and I wonder if my stomach can take it.

Gryff nods. 'Next stop Morgelyn.'

Soon we're scudding over the waves. The spray wets my face and tangles my hair, and when I lick my lips, I taste salt. I feel flooded by it all, the winter sun, the air, the colours: slate grey and royal blue, frothing white and emerald green. Rocky islets and skerries stick up out of the water like the fingers of giants. Was that one of Davy's stories?

'This bit of water's The Road,' Gryff shouts. 'Stretches from the North Channel up to Crow Sound. And over there's Samson and Bryher . . .'

His voice merges with the wind, until I somehow hear Davy's voice instead, reciting the names of the islands like a spell: *An Nor, Samson, Breghyek, Pennpras, Treskaw, Rag's Ledge, Paper Ledge, Crow Point*. I close my eyes, feeling dizzy.

'And there she is,' Gryff says. 'Morgelyn.'

I open my eyes. Up ahead, an island rises out of the sea, darker green than the others around it, encircled by grey rocks. And in a flash, I remember seeing it for the first time, the way my mother held me tightly, her brown eyes wide and her dark curls tossed by the sea air.

Look, Mina! Our new home.

'You've not been here for some time, I think.'

I look back to find Gryff watching me.

'No.' I clear my throat. 'Not since I was a kid. I spent a few months here.'

'I remember.' His eyes crinkle. 'You were a funny little thing.'

I look at him in surprise, but he doesn't say more, only brings the boat up alongside a weathered grey jetty and chucks a rope up to secure it, cinching us to a ladder.

'Thank you for the lift,' I say, as the noise of the motor dies away. 'Do I owe you anything?'

He shakes his head. 'Welcome back, Miss Kestle.'

Lost for words, I scramble up the ladder and walk away, my heels thudding hollow on the old planks of the jetty.

No roads on Morgelyn, that's the first thing I remember as I step onto the shore. No streetlights either, no signposts, no cars – only sandy paths that lead always to the sea. Even though it's Saturday morning, there isn't a soul around, and for a bewildering moment it's as if I've stepped onto a stage set, pulled from my memories.

There's the stand of low fishermen's cottages, their gates opening right onto the pebbly shore, festive wreaths of shells and sea holly and ivy decorating their front doors. There's the deeply weathered, rusted red phone box I reached from London. There's the tiny village shop, its windows a riot of coloured lights, and there's the ramshackle pub, all peeling whitewash and balding, roped-down thatch, an upturned boat in the front garden.

I walk towards it, as if in a dream. The closer I get, the more dilapidated it looks, the sign so faded and battered that I can barely read it.

The Helm Inn

I stop. The pub's door stands ajar, a warm, rich smell of roasting apples and buttery pastry spiralling out towards me. My stomach wakes up and lets out a loud protest of hunger, chiding me for ignoring the custard creams. I peer around, but there's no such thing as an 'Open' sign.

'Hello?' I call.

There's no answer, apart from a distant clatter of pans. Hesitantly, I push the door open and step inside.

It takes a while for my eyes to adjust, filled as they are with silver sea-light. Slowly, details emerge. Sandy flagstones, exposed beams hung with mismatched baubles and old dried hops, uneven walls decorated with postcards and sea charts from all over the world. A deep stone fireplace takes up one whole wall, driftwood smouldering in the grate.

'All right, Clive,' a voice calls, and the door behind the bar swings open. 'I'll serve you *one*, but after that you have to . . . oh.'

A woman stops dead at the sight of me. She's wearing oven gloves, a tray in her arms filled with what look like pasties, still steaming from the oven. She's younger than me, her cropped curly black hair held back with a bright yellow scarf, a riot of tattoos covering each arm.

'Help you?' she asks.

'I wasn't sure if you were open . . .'

'Technically not,' she says, shoving the tray onto the side.

'Oh. Well, don't worry—'

'I'm joking. Sit down.' She waves me onto a stool. 'What are you after? Coffee? Or something stronger?'

I'm almost tempted by the latter, after my morning. 'Coffee, please.'

She moves around the bar with practised ease, flicking on a kettle, filling a cafetière.

'Here to check out the cottage?'

I glance at her sharply, but her back is to me. All I can make out is the tattoo of a flock of birds that disappears beneath her faded sweatshirt.

'Yes,' I say hesitantly, before remembering that this place is so small, news must travel faster than light. 'Just for the day. I caught the night train down.'

'You've been to see Leticia already?'

'I have.'

When she turns back, her face is serious. 'Davy trusts you, you know. Don't let him down.'

A flash of anger goes through me again, but before I can say *he doesn't even know me*, she's gone, pulling her phone from her pocket and striding away through the kitchen doors.

I stare after her, expecting her to come back at any moment, but she doesn't. Eventually, I pour the coffee and take a sip of the bitter brew, trying to shove away a flicker of hurt. This is a small place. Of course they're going to be wary of newcomers.

The tray of freshly baked pasties are where she left them, steaming softly. I stare at that golden-brown pastry, caught between embarrassment and hunger, until hunger wins out.

'Excuse me?' I call.

There's no reply from the kitchen.

Surely they're for sale ...? Before I can change my mind, I grab one up, leave a ten-pound note under my cup, and hurry out of the door.

I take a deep breath of the chill air, striding towards the dunes as quickly as I can in my heels, the pastry hot in my hands.

I should have known this wouldn't be easy. A community like this is tight-knit and I'm an outsider, stumbling through the complex knots of relationships and friendships woven over decades, if not centuries. By rights, I shouldn't even be here.

Absent-mindedly, I take a bite of the pasty and taste rich, festive spices – cinnamon, ginger, cloves – and sweet winter apples, brandy-soaked raisins, the pastry tinted with saffron. I make a mess as I walk, but I don't care, and soon I'm cramming the last thick knot into my mouth, leaving a trail of crumbs for the birds.

Reaching a crossroads at the edge of the village, I stop. A sandy path runs right, a wider one leads straight on, and to the left a narrow track cuts into the thick gorse, winding a way over the dunes. Even though it has been twenty years, I know without a doubt which one to take.

My high heels sink into the sand until finally I give up and take them off, wiggling my toes with relief. As I climb, the land changes, sand becoming gritty soil, gorse and heather growing higher around me until, finally, I crest the headland and find myself on what must be the highest point of the island, empty and windswept.

I stop to catch my breath, blood racing through my body, the wind whipping strands of my hair. From here, I can see how small Morgelyn truly is, a haven of scattered houses and postage-stamp-sized fields, rocky outcrops and secret coves and, above everything, the sky – so vast that it doesn't look real – like a huge oil painting pinned to the horizon.

A shiver runs through me as I look around. I am utterly alone, nothing but the gorse and the birds and the wild roar of the Atlantic.

This is a place beyond time. I might be a hundred years in the past, a thousand, beneath the same sky.

Rubbing my arms, I carry on down the path as it slopes through thick furze, the sound of waves growing louder until, finally, I'm there.

Davy's cottage stands alone in a tiny cove, sheltered by banks of gorse and bracken. Its grey stone walls are so worn by the winds they're almost round, the slate roof thick with lichen, the glass studio built onto the side overgrown with brambles and heather. The garden is the cove itself, a crescent of pebbles and white sand. And beyond, open sea.

Trembling with something more than cold, I take a step forward and I remember how I had clung to my mother's hand, how cold her fingers were, even through my mittens. I remember how the front door of the cottage flew open, and how a man stepped out, a pen in one hand, a look of utter surprise on his face. I remember the grey cat who twined around him, before trotting forwards to sniff my outstretched hand as my mother laughed and said, *Merry Christmas, Davy.*

I blink. Now, the blue-painted door is shut tight, faded and peeling, and there is no one to greet me. Worse, the more I look, the more I see the changes twenty years have wrought. One of the cottage's windows is broken, patched with wood. The pots of herbs and flowers are full of weeds, brown stalks left to wither, the roof gap-toothed with missing slates. A large stone bowl stands empty beside the doorstep.

'Hello?' I call. The sea answers me, with its endless *hussssh.*

Gripping the key, I pick my way down the path. Strings of shells and driftwood spin and clink gently from the eaves of the cottage. Despite what Leticia said, it feels wrong to let myself in, or to be here at all.

Come in, Davy had cried, when I was a child. *Come inside and get warm.* And I had marvelled at the cottage, so different to our suburban house back home. A stone fireplace with bright copper pots, a deep window seat with faded curtains and squashy cushions. A wooden table, scrubbed to whiteness, a stone floor covered in thin, sandy rugs, a worn armchair where the big grey cat jumped up to settle before the hearth. The smell of smoke and sea, baked bread and paint and the sweetness of old, old wood . . .

Mustering my courage, I fit the key to the lock and shove the door open.

The memory fades. The place feels damp, cold, abandoned. There's no fire in the grate, no hot chocolate on the stove, no cat in the armchair.

And all at once, I feel more alone than I ever have in my life. More than when a police officer sat me down in my father's lounge in the middle of the night and asked if I understood what he was telling me about my mother, more than when my father drove away from the boarding school, leaving me in a smart uniform that smelled new and not of home. More than when all my letters to my godfather went unanswered . . .

A sob breaks from me and I clap a hand to my mouth.

What am I doing here?

I pull the envelope from my bag, intending to leave, when something white flutters to the floor.

The note. Impossible that something so small should be enough to upend my life, to send me running back into a past I thought lost. Impossible that, after twenty years of silence, all it took was five small words:

Mina – please look after her.

CHAPTER FIVE

'Cat?' I call, swiping the tears from my face. 'Are you here?' Hugging my jacket around me, I tiptoe through the cottage. It's just as I remember, only smaller: the same shelves stuffed higgledy-piggledy with books, their pages plumped by the salty air, the old ship's lantern hanging from the beam, the mantel crowded with shells and sea glass and trinkets. I pick up a little figurine carved from driftwood. It's abstract, but I make out what could be a cat, leaping high over the waves. I set it back and run my fingers across the rough surface of the mantel.

Did I ever tell you, Mina, the story of this beam? It came from a ship, hundreds of years ago, a ship that was wrecked in a storm. You see, my great-great-great-grandfather was a sailor, going to trade in Penzance . . .

I shake my head to clear it of the memory of Davy's voice and turn away.

The little kitchen is at the back of the cottage. An old gas stove, wooden sideboards and a deep stone sink. Beside it, a hard bar of soap and a single plate, cup and spoon upon the rack.

'Oh, Davy,' I whisper.

*

'Bramble jam!' he called from the table.

I stood on tiptoe on the counter, staring up at the shelves. 'Four jars.'

'Good. Hawthorn jelly?'

'Three jars.'

'Pickled winkles?'

'Um, two jars and this is pick . . . pickled cabbage?'

'Yuck! That's from Mrs Pounce, must have been there ten years – all right, sea buckthorn in syrup?'

'Two!'

'Check!'

I beamed down from the counter. On the highest shelf above my head, three jars stood alone.

'What are these?'

Davy smiled from the table, his hair wild with spray, the list in front of him growing as we planned our Christmas feast. 'Gorse blossom honey. Gryff makes it every year when his bees come to visit the gorse.'

He stood up and took down a jar, unscrewing the lid with his gnarled hands, holding it out to me to sniff. The honey inside was pure gold, brighter than any honey I'd ever seen. It smelled different, too, like salt and caramel and roses.

'Smells strange.'

'That's because it's special. Made from island flowers that dance with the sea. You understand?'

I nodded, though I hadn't.

'All right,' Davy said, sitting down again with a grunt. 'Pickled sea beet?'

I turn away from the kitchen, feeling like a visitor in some strange, forgotten museum. On that first day as a child, I had run through every single one of the cottage's five rooms, fascinated and delighted by the lean-to bathroom with its claw-footed bath and terrifying, rattling gas boiler; by the room that was to be mine – while Mum and I looked for a place to live – its bed built from an old rowing boat; by Davy's studio . . . Holding my breath, I push the door open.

This was the room I loved most. Not even a real room, more like a homemade conservatory of mismatched window frames, built onto the side of the house. Over the years, heather and gorse have grown up the sides, creeping through gaps in the wood, until it's as much outside as in. The sea fills the panes with blue, so much blue.

I breathe in the scent of dust and turpentine. A canvas stands on an easel, blank save for a few hesitant charcoal lines – a painting Davy might never return to. Papers litter every surface, stubs of pencils, bits of string. A reference book remains open: *Cornish Myths and Legends*. Lying across it is a handwritten note on a piece of paper.

She'll be here when the gorse flowers

A fragment from one of Davy's stories? I let it fall back onto the desk. Perhaps his mind was wandering.

Back in the main room, I flump into an armchair, a cloud of dust and dander rising up around me. What do I do now? How am I supposed to look after a cat I can't even find?

Something creaks in the cottage and I freeze, realising abruptly just how alone I am here.

'Cat?' I call, pushing myself up in the chair. There's a scuffle again, closer this time, the sound of stone knocking against stone. It's coming from the front door. Mouth dry, I creep my way across the flagstones, reach for the door and fling it open.

A flurry of fur, a flash of green and a grey shape skitters off around the side of the cottage, paws scattering sand.

'Cat!' I call, tripping after it, throwing myself around the corner. 'Wait!'

I collide heavily with a figure so abruptly that a shriek escapes me, brain scrambling in fright, telling me to run even as I struggle to keep my footing. Grabbing the wall, I look up into the face of a stranger.

The man stares back, and some of my fear ebbs away as I realise he looks just as startled as I do, until I see the metal file in his hand. There are flakes of paint and splinters of wood on his cuff and one of the studio's windows looks damaged. He's clearly been trying to jimmy it open . . .

'What the hell do you think you're doing?'

The words break from me, rough with anger and alarm.

The man takes a step back. He's a few years older than me, perhaps, a dark beard covering his cheeks, thick, black curls tangled with salt spray.

He holds up his hands as if guilty, still clutching the file. 'This isn't—'

'What it looks like? Because it looks like you were trying to break in.'

'No, I . . .'

I grab for my phone. 'I'm calling the police.'

'I just came to feed the cat!'

The words stop me in my tracks.

'What?'

'The cat.' The man raises a dark brow. 'Davy's cat, Murr. I came to feed her, but I haven't seen her for days, and I can't find the key. So I thought I'd try and get in another way.' He waggles the file. 'Are you still going to call the police?'

The vague amusement in his voice makes my cheeks flame. 'What's your name?' I demand, as coolly as I can.

He tucks the file into one pocket of his oilskin jacket. 'Jem Fletcher. I'm Davy's neighbour.'

Jem. The name is familiar. 'You're the one who found Davy?'

The man nods, squinting out to sea. 'I was out looking for driftwood and passed by the rocks just east of here. That's when I heard Murr, yelling and yelling. So I came down and saw him lying there.' He shakes his head.

'Well, thank you,' I tell him awkwardly. 'For Davy, and for … looking after the cat.' The phone is still in my hand, from when I threatened to call the police. 'Sorry. I was just surprised.'

He smiles, a little mockingly. 'You would have had a job getting the police here, anyway. Most of them are at the school carol concert.'

For a moment neither of us speaks, caught up in the absence of Davy Penhallow, in the traces of him everywhere: the green waders hanging on a nail, the painted stones and shells that litter the pots around the cottage. An old, familiar wave of loneliness starts to swell in me again. I push it away. *Just do what you came here to do, and leave.*

I look at Jem. He could be the answer to my cat-sitting dilemma, if I can persuade him.

'I'm Mina,' I say, holding out my hand with what I hope is a friendly smile.

He takes in my shoeless feet, my crumpled party attire. 'I know.'

For a second I think he'll leave my hand hanging, but then he holds out his own, keeping his distance. I shake it. His fingers are rough and callused, chilled by the sea spray.

'Would you like a cup of tea?' I ask.

Jem frowns at me suspiciously, before glancing at the cottage. 'All right.'

He follows me inside, only for a dried sprig of sea holly above the door to catch in his dark hair.

'Every time,' he mutters, disentangling it.

I turn towards the kitchen, and immediately realise that, despite my invitation, I don't remember where anything is. 'Ah ...'

Jem brushes past me. 'Here.'

I watch as he fills the kettle and places it on the gas stove, lighting it with practised ease, before taking a tin of tea leaves and a carton of long-life milk from a cupboard. He makes no attempt at small talk, as if I were some random stranger.

Aren't you? a small voice asks.

Ignoring it, I put on another smile. 'So you've been feeding the cat?'

Jem snorts. 'That old lady can feed herself. But yes, I've been bringing her food. Haven't seen hide nor hair of her since they took Davy away, though.'

I glance out of the window, hoping to see a grey fluffy head pop up from the heather, but there's nothing, just the purple flowers stirring in the breeze. 'I think I saw her just now. But she ran away.'

'Wouldn't you, if you saw an intruder in your house?'

I bite back a gasp of disbelief at his rudeness. His whole presence seems to radiate distrust, as if I've personally wronged him.

Stepping away, I take a breath. I don't need him to like me. And I don't ever have to see him again after this.

The kettle's insistent whistle fills the kitchen. I hear Jem take it off the stove, hear the gurgle of water being poured into a pot.

'Listen.' I make my voice calm. 'I don't want to cause trouble. I have no idea why Davy sent me the key, or why he wants me to look after his cat, after all this time ...' To my surprise and embarrassment, my throat tightens. I clear it and go on. 'But

I'm not staying. I just came to see that everything was being taken care of.'

Jem doesn't look at me as he puts the lid on the teapot. 'Davy must have had his reasons.'

'Well, if he did, he didn't bother to share them.'

'More like you couldn't be bothered to find out.'

'What's that supposed to mean?'

'You know what it means.' He finally looks at me, utterly accusing. 'You never cared while he was well, but you're quick enough to come running now that he's at death's door.'

I stare at him. The words bring heat to my eyes, as if I've scalded myself.

'How dare you,' I choke. 'You don't know anything about it.'

'I know more than you think.' He strides towards the door, taking a newspaper-wrapped package from his jacket and tossing it down on the table as he goes. 'That's for Murr. *If* you can be bothered to give it to her.'

Before I can summon up a retort, he drags open the door and is gone.

I shove the second cup back into the cupboard and pour the tea, trying to warm myself with the heat of anger. Who the hell does he think he is, to speak to me like that?

Someone who knows Davy. Someone who isn't a stranger here.

I lean on the sink, staring at the heather beyond the window.

Is he right? Davy was the one to cut off contact with me all those years ago, ignoring every single letter I sent until, as a heartbroken eight-year-old, I had to admit I had been abandoned. It's true, I never tried to patch things up with him after that. But why should I have, when his silence made it so clear he wanted nothing to do with me? My reflection hovers in the glass, and abruptly I see myself as I was, twenty years ago. Before I can push it away, the memory comes flooding back . . .

I sat on the wooden kitchen counter, breathing in the cottage's smell: pungent greenery, smoke from the hearth, wet sand from our wellingtons and rich hot chocolate steaming as my mother prepared the mugs, humming along to a carol on the crackling radio.

When I looked up, the wrinkles at the corners of Davy's eyes were creased deep in a smile. 'Finished,' he said.

I scrambled around on my knees to look at my reflection in the dark window. A crown of heather and sea holly and bright yellow gorse flowers sat on my hair.

'I look like a fairy!'

'More like a sea maiden,' my mum teased. Her dark hair was crowned with sea holly too, her cheeks pinked.

'Like the one in your stories?' I asked Davy.

'That's right,' Davy said, reaching up to hang a new branch of sea holly above the front door. 'Like Morgelyn, who watches over us, as we watch over her land.'

'And her cat?' I asked.

'And her cat.'

He performed a respectful bow to the huge grey cat who sprawled on the hearthrug, belly out to the flames, fast asleep.

'Was Murr really there when Lyonesse flooded?'

'She was.' Davy nudged Murr with his slippered toe. The cat woke with a chirrup of surprise and opened her green eyes. 'Murr here is no normal cat. She holds the power of storms in her tail. How else could she have challenged the sea itself?'

I stared hard. 'She doesn't look very powerful.'

'That's because she's also exceptionally lazy.' Davy took a trailing length of ribbon and dangled it in front of Murr's nose. 'Wake up, oh mighty one.'

Murr took a lazy swipe at the ribbon, and my laughter filled the little cottage, so warm and cosy on a Christmas night.

My face looks back at me from the glass, a smile fading into a frown as I banish the memory, like so many others. With a sigh, I walk to the open front door. 'Murr?' I call, across the beach, listening to the low *hiss* of the waves and the distant roar of the Atlantic.

Nothing. I close the door and retreat to my cup of tea, hugging the warmth of it to my chest. As I drink, I try to calm down by looking at the prints and photographs and posters that crowd the walls. One advertises an exhibition of Davy's work at a local gallery on St Martin's, another is a very old photograph of the cottage, blurred figures standing around a boat on the beach. Another is a newspaper article from around ten years ago, showing Davy posing self-consciously beside a group of young people. One of them catches my eye: messy black curls, wide smile. Jem Fletcher.

Mr Penhallow with this summer's
Cornish Art School students.

I turn away with a scowl and find myself looking at a bare patch of wall. Abruptly, I remember what used to hang here. One of my mother's photographs – the one she gave Davy that Christmas, in a specially made wooden frame. It was a photo of the cottage, taken on a summer's eve, the building almost lost in a golden haze. I remember how Davy had made a fuss and hung it in pride of place. Now there's nothing but an empty nail. I search the other frames, but it's nowhere.

Gone. Forgotten about. Like me.

Perhaps that's how it should stay. My memories of this place may be bright, but they're few, like fairy lights in the darkness. They belong to a child, not to the woman I am now, who goes to bed stressing over deliverables and client satisfaction. Who zipped her dreams up in a fraying art portfolio and shoved them under the bed, to be forgotten.

Decisively, I empty the teapot and wash the cup, place it carefully to drain.

The newspaper-wrapped packet is on the table where Fletcher left it.

Opening it, I see a filleted fish; so fresh it still smells of the sea. I drop the whole lot into the stone bowl that waits beside the front step. I don't see what else I can do. And anyway, didn't Fletcher say he was feeding Murr? If so, I've done my duty.

Slinging my coat around myself, I jam my feet back into the heels and step through the door, locking it behind me, the winter wind stinging my wet face.

At the edge of the path, I turn back.

For an instant, I think I see a face looking out at me from the cottage's window but when I blink it's gone.

Just the shadow of a passing sea bird.

CHAPTER SIX

D*id I ever tell you, Mina, how my grandfather found his way to this island? Not my nearest grandfather, you understand, another one, many grandfathers back, so far back that his name has been worn away by the tides.*

His story began on another Midwinter's Eve, when the sea was in one of its rages and could not be calmed by song or by sail. A bad night to be abroad, and yet on the headland stood a young woman, drenched to the skin, her cloak whipping about her, watching the waves for a sign of life, for a ship's lantern drowning like a firefly in the storm.

The cry had gone up an hour earlier, cutting through the midwinter celebrations at the inn, bellowed above music and merriment.

Wreck! Wreck!

Lightning tore the sky and timbers groaned on the wild seas as a ship broke apart on the rocks. The girl was frozen and she was scared, and when lightning tore the sky again, she turned away to hurry home – wreck or no wreck, survivors or no survivors. But she hadn't made it three paces when a shape leaped from the gorse into her path, a creature of smoke and shadow, with eyes like marsh fire. It looked like a cat, but the girl was not fooled, for she knew a sea spirit when she saw one.

The priest would have told her to call upon God, but the priest was not from the islands. Never cross a spirit, that's what her grandma always said. And so she did the only thing she could think of: she lowered her head and bowed to the creature.

In return, it blinked and trotted away, tail raised as if summoning her to follow.

And so she did, trailing the cat spirit through the secret passages in the gorse, all the way down to the shore, where waves smashed the rocks and rain lashed the sand, deafening, blinding. And though her eyes stung with salt, she peered into the darkness and saw a shape bobbing in the water. Something long and wooden with a sack lashed upon it. Not a sack, she realised in horror, a person.

'Man in the water!' she screamed. 'Man alive!'

But none heard her, battling with boats and their own consciences as they watched the wreck founder out on the waves. The young woman turned, desperate, and when the cat spirit let out a cry, its voice as loud as the storm, she knew what to do.

She let her cloak fall to the sand, kicked off her boots, unlaced her dress with numb fingers and ran into the freezing surf in her shift. The sea shoved her back and spat spray at her, but she was young and she was strong and she was island-born. She waded deep, then swam and swam and even though the icy waves stole her breath and froze her hands, she finally caught hold of the shipwrecked man's jacket and heaved him towards the shore until, at last, she felt sand beneath her feet and knew they would be safe.

Up on the strand she rolled him over, and by the light of a storm-tossed moon, she saw his face. Dark curls, skin the colour of fine rosewood. Gold rings upon his fingers and gold buttons on his coat. A Barbary trader, sailing to Penzance with his scarlet cloth and spices and wine from across the sea. And when he did not breathe, she rolled him onto his front and pummelled his back until he came alive and coughed out water by the gallon.

'Tu qui star?' he croaked when he could speak, and she recognised the words as Sabir, the sailor's language.

'Mi star amigo,' she said. 'I'm a friend.'

Movement flickered at the corner of her eye; the cat spirit, summoning her towards a hollow in the furze.

And so she helped the shipwrecked man into that shelter of bracken, and strangers though they were, they held each other tight beneath her cloak, and the cat spirit curled beside them, purring them warm, singing through the wild hours of the night.

When they woke it was to a clear blue sky and a calm blue sea and the spirit was just a cat after all, washing itself in the pale morning sun.

The girl laughed, and so did the man, and in time he became the girl's husband and in time they built this cottage.

And this mantel above the fire, Mina? It's the mast from his foundered ship. And the cat who saved him . . .?

'Stories,' I whisper to myself, staring at what is unmistakably a cave in the bracken, a snug, secret shelter where a woman and a man might once have found refuge from the elements. A tuft of grey fur is caught in the woody old growth. I touch it gently, only for the wind to pluck it from my fingers and bear it away over the dunes.

Standing, I wipe my eyes. 'Children's stories.'

Still, as I crest the headland, Davy's words seem so real. There, the rocks where the ship was wrecked, here, the place where a girl once kept watch in the night. I shiver. This place is getting to me, working itself into my skin just as it did when I was a child, until I cried when I had to leave.

Only for a week, Mum had consoled me. She couldn't have known it would end up being decades.

Shouldering my bag, I hurry down towards the pub. Even though it's barely mid-afternoon, the daylight is fading fast, turning purple-grey as the bloom of a sloe. Clouds roil on the horizon in fantastical shapes, and the wind is picking up. I check my phone and feel a flutter of anxiety: even though Leticia said I had plenty of time, I've stayed longer than I meant to and I still need to get back to St Mary's.

The island seems more alive now, children playing on the shore, smoke puffing from the chimneys. A group of people stand around next to the pub, staring at a sign driven into the ground. They all turn to look as I walk up, my heels scuffing the path, but I ignore them, striding through the front door.

It's busier now, at least in comparison with earlier. Two older women are playing darts, a middle-aged man with big round glasses is ensconced in a window seat with a book and a mug of tea, and a bald man in tweed is hunched at the end of the bar, nursing a pint of bitter and slowly knitting what looks like a Babygro for a squid. The whole place smells of mulled wine and baked apples and woodsmoke, jaunty Christmas songs playing on the radio, and for a second, all I want to do is sink into that cosy atmosphere.

'Back again?' the young woman calls from the bar. 'Enjoy the pasty?'

I raise my chin and take the key from my pocket with as much dignity as I can. 'Yes, thank you. Can I leave this with you? In case Leticia needs it, or ...' Heat floods my face at the memory of the rude man, Jem Fletcher. 'Or anyone else. Until Davy comes back.'

The woman raises a dark brow. 'You're leaving?'

'I have to get back to London. Do you know if there's a water taxi to St Mary's?'

'En't no taxis in winter,' the man at the bar observes to his knitting.

I force a smile. 'All right, then. What about the person who brought me over? Gryff or Gruff I think his name was?'

The young woman leans over her shoulder to bellow into the kitchen. 'Gramps!'

'I am *not* taking those salmon,' comes the yelled response. 'I don't care how cheap Lucas goes—' The old man stops in the doorway, a white chef's apron over his clumsily knitted jumper. 'Hello, Miss Kestle!' he beams. 'Staying for dinner? Good menu tonight, bass with meunière sauce and steamed rock samphire, and I've got a batch of chocolate orange brownies on the go.'

'No, thank you, I have to get back for my flight. Could you take me over?'

'Me?' The man's eyes are as round as the pickled eggs in the jars behind him. 'Oh, I'm sorry, Miss Kestle, but I'm midway through a sauce.'

'Someone else, then?' There's silence. 'I'll pay, of course.'

Gryff rubs at his grey stubble. 'How about it, Sylvia?' he calls to one of the women playing darts.

'Sorry, mate,' she shrugs. 'I'm half cut.'

'What about Lucas?'

'Nope. He's babysitting for Lila tonight.'

'We could ask Jem,' the young woman says with mock innocence. My expression must darken, because she laughs. 'Although it looks like you've already met my brother.'

'Your brother?' I ask flatly. Now she's said it, I can see a slight resemblance, in the dark curls, the set of her jaw.

'Elodie,' Gryff chides gently, and I realise that Jem must have already gossiped to half the island about me. 'You'd be much better off waiting till tomorrow, Miss Kestle,' Gryff goes on. 'Stay here tonight, have a good feed, and we'll hop across bright and early.'

Maybe it's the knowledge that everyone's been talking, or

the young woman's smirk, but I grip my handbag and turn on my heel.

'Thanks, but I need to catch a flight.'

As the pub door swings shut behind me, I hear them all burst into whispers. Face burning, I stride over to the village shop but it seems to be shut, even though the lights are on. Next, I try the jetty only to find a faded, out-of-date summer timetable flapping from a nail.

I pull out my phone and try a search, but no combination of 'water taxi' or 'ferry' and 'St Mary's' will give me anything useful. Digging in my pocket for Leticia's card, I dial her number, only to be greeted by her cheery voicemail, telling me to leave a message. It's a similar story when I find a number for Scilly Air Transfers.

Finally, in utter frustration, I call Paola.

'Mina!' She's somewhere crowded – a café, maybe, or the Christmas market. 'At last. I thought you'd drowned.'

Her voice is so familiar, so carefree, that I press the phone to my ear, wishing I could sink through the screen and emerge where she is, somewhere bustling and busy.

'Sorry, patchy signal.' I grip my coat as the wind buffets me. 'P, you will not believe what's happened.'

With the wind muttering in my ear and my fingers slowly freezing around my phone, I tell her about my day; about meeting Leticia and seeing Davy in the hospital, the strange guardianship he's seemingly bestowed upon me, the cottage and my run-in with Jem Fletcher, and the mysterious cat.

'And now I can't find anyone to take me back to the main island. I'm stuck.'

'*Cavolo*. What are you going to do?'

'I don't know!' Closing my eyes, I remember Gryff's friendly manner. 'There's a pub here. I guess I could stay the night and get another flight tomorrow.'

'Why not? It's the weekend.' Paola sounds distracted, ordering a drink from someone. 'Make sure you're back in time for work on Monday, though. Big meeting. And Marianne will want to go over your presentation to Hunter-Thorpe.'

'Of course I will be.'

'OK. And Mina, send me pictures!'

By the time I end the call and look up from my phone, the sky has turned navy blue at the edges. I snap a photo of the moody scene and hit send.

A reply comes back almost immediately.

Nice. Now go get wine.

I smile. Suddenly, the idea of taking a tiny boat across those inky, choppy waves doesn't seem so appealing after all.

Steeling myself, I walk back into the cosy pub.

'Here she is again,' Gryff cries, as if they've all been waiting. 'So what'll it be, bird? Sole or sea bass? Or are you vegan? I do a smashing tofu cutlet with cranberry sauce.'

Even my professional smile, so well practised, is hard to find. 'Could I just get a room, please?'

'Oh. Oh dear, no. I'm afraid we don't rent rooms in the winter.'

'Can't afford to,' the young woman shrugs, wiping the bar.

I stare at them. They're having me on, I'm sure of it. The back of my neck grows hot beneath the collective gaze of the pub.

'But you said I should stay.'

'Bless you, I didn't mean here!' Gryff smiles encouragingly. 'I meant out at Davy's place. He'd throw a fit if he heard I put you in one of these damp old rooms. He'd want you to stay at the cottage. He's waited long enough for you to come.'

'I'm not staying there.' The words are out of my mouth before I know I've said them. 'I can't.'

'Why not? Here.' He pushes the key back into my hand. 'But stay, have dinner first, take a look at the menu . . .'

I know it's rude, but I can't stand it any more – the scrutiny, the mockery, the current of unsaid words that I can feel but not grasp. And I hear Jem's voice again, the scorn and disappointment as he accused me of ignoring Davy until he was ill.

I march back into the night, ignoring Gryff's voice as he calls after me.

By the time I reach the crest of the hill again, it's fully dark. Below, the pub is a pool of golden light, sparking on the waves, and abruptly I wish I'd stayed, laughed off my bad mood and washed it down with brownies and hot, spiced wine. With a sigh, I let my head fall back, only to catch my breath.

Stars spill across the sky above me, numberless, brilliant, like a million scattered diamonds. I crane my neck, trying to take them all in, trying to see more, and out of nowhere I'm laughing, my breath misting in the cold air, because the sky is so vast, so beautiful that it barely makes sense.

Finally, I have to look down again, eyes swimming with stars, neck aching, only to realise I can't see a thing. The island is dark in a way I've never known. Not city darkness, glowing red with taillights and streetlamps, but real darkness, deep enough to fall into. I fumble out my phone and turn on the torch.

The gorse is stark in the white light, casting strange, clawed shadows across the path. My footsteps suddenly seem very loud and lonely among the endless bracken.

Don't be stupid. It's just a thicket. Not even a very big one. There's nothing that could hurt you.

But Davy's stories come coiling into my mind. Tales of buccas, who tangle fishing nets and pull fishermen down with their webbed fingers and sad, lobster eyes. Of drowned men and phantom ships, of the spirits that dance on the wind and whisper down the chimney on midwinter nights . . .

These islands are full of ghosts, Mina. They're all around us, echoes of those who went before. They're here, singing, if we only learn how to hear them.

A stick cracks and I turn, eyes flooding.

'Hello?' I call, my voice weak.

Another crack and I can't help it; I break into a run, barging through the heather, stumbling in my ridiculous shoes. Gorse snatches at my hair, pulling it from the band, but I plough on, the torchlight bouncing madly, turning the shadows into rearing beasts.

Something catches at my ankle and I trip, crashing heavily onto the path, my phone skittering away.

There's a rustle and I look up. The silver eyes of an animal watch from the shadows of the gorse.

'Murr?' I whisper.

The shape whisks away into the bracken. Scrambling up and grabbing my phone, I follow, and within a few steps, I realise I'm already at the cove, the sand glowing in the starlight.

This time, when I open the door, a soft, grey shadow appears out of nowhere and brushes against my shins to slip inside, making my skin leap.

Inside is just as dark as out. By phone torch, I find matches and light the stove, followed by the old ship's lantern that hangs from the beam, the way I remember Davy used to. The wick sputters into life, and I turn the brass dial until the whole cottage glows, like the inside of a jar of honey.

Green flashes and I turn, looking straight into a pair of bright eyes. For a moment, my ears roar as if I'm underwater, the cottage around me seems to shift, turning to smoke, and I'm sure I can smell icy air and freshly cut greenery, stolen spices, salt water and

sea holly; I'm sure I hear someone singing, an old, old song ...
Then just as quickly as it rose, the sensation fades. I'm looking at a
cat, an ordinary, long-haired grey cat, with strikingly green eyes.
She seems a little worse for wear, thin beneath her fluffy coat, fur
matted in places, bits of dead foliage caught in the clumps. But
apart from that, she looks just as I remember. She *can't* be the
same cat, can she? She'd be ancient. More than twenty.

'Murr?' I greet hesitantly.

Blinking haughtily, the cat turns away, looking rather pointedly at the cold fireplace. Shivering, I kneel down beside the
hearth. There are bits of driftwood and old planks in the basket,
a few twigs for kindling. How hard can it be?

I try to recall how Mum and I used to do it, crouching in
our dressing gowns and slippers on those cold winter mornings,
delighted by this big old stone hearth, nothing like the gas fire I
grew up with and its plastic coals. I remember scrunching balls
of newspaper, stacking up the logs ...

Holding my breath, I light the paper with a match. It flares
brightly, beautifully, but all too soon it's lost to ash. The second
attempt works better and finally the kindling catches and the
driftwood begins to spark until a fire crackles weakly in the grate.

I sit back on my heels and smile triumphantly at Murr. She
looks at me with narrowed eyes, the flames dancing and casting
shadows in those pools of green.

Hesitantly, I reach out a hand towards her, but she pulls her
head away.

'Don't you remember me?' I ask.

She doesn't move, but she stays wary, watching. For some
reason, her mistrust hurts more than Jem's words, or the laughter
of the people in the pub. 'I'm sorry about Davy,' I tell her.

At his name, she seems to soften a little, sinking down.

'Are you hungry?' I ask. 'Did you find the fish?'

Getting up, I inch open the front door, scared to let the night in. The stone bowl is empty, except for a few bits of bone and scale. A memory stirs, of Davy standing with the night at his back, a bottle of milk in his hand.

'*We mustn't forget to fill the bowl at night, Mina.*' He winked. '*The sea spirits are always hungry, but if there's milk for them, they'll drink their fill and keep us safe.*'

'*Davy.*' Mum laughed, looking through some negatives beside the fire. '*You'll scare her.*'

'*I'm not scared,*' I boasted, before peering at the bowl. '*Will Murr drink it?*'

Davy just shrugged. '*If she does, that's her right.*'

I tear my gaze away. Just another story, like so many Davy told to keep me entertained. Still . . . what can it hurt? Murr probably drank it then and will drink it now. I take the long-life milk from the counter and splash some into the stone bowl.

'There,' I tell Murr, pouring a little more into a saucer, and placing it down on the hearth. 'Now we're safe.'

With a sort of huffing sound, she creeps forward to investigate the milk. I stay very still, and soon, a steady lapping fills the room.

Sinking back into the armchair, I pull out my phone to message Paola, only to discover that there's no signal.

Of course. Alone, in a spooky cottage, with no signal and just a cat for company.

I rub at my face. I should have organised the return boat trip before, should have planned better, but at the same time, Gryff's words come back to me.

He would want you to stay. He's waited long enough for you to come.

It's just for a night. And the cottage doesn't feel quite so lonely any more, with the fire lit and Murr washing her face beside me.

Eight-year-old Mina was happy here. So was Mum. Maybe remembering that isn't so bad, after all this time.

'A toast,' Mum said, raising her glass. 'To the time of year that brings wandering feet home.'

'And to those who guide our steps through the darkness,' Davy replied, smiling down at Murr.

The liquid in the glass was apricot-orange, almost glowing. I held my own, a thimble-full, and took a sip. It was strong and sour-sweet and made me stick my tongue out in disgust.

'Seaberry wine,' Davy laughed. 'My own invention.'

Pushing myself from the armchair, I pad over to the huge old dresser that stands against one wall, so big it must have been built inside the cottage, made to fit. The top is a cabinet, with little panes of blown glass, holding bubbles like seawater. Inside are treasures; not silver or crystal, but perfect shells, fossils, feathers, strange objects tumbled by the waves, flotsam and jetsam from four corners of the world, washed up on this tiny island at the edge of the fierce Atlantic.

I kneel down and open the cupboard. It smells of soft old wood and ancient linen, but there, resting on their sides, are the bottles. I pull one out and hold it to the light. It swirls, pink-orange as sunset.

Tugging out the cork, I pour a little into a mug. 'To the past,' I say, raising it to Murr. She blinks and for an instant, I see figures reflected in her bright eyes.

Quickly, I take a sip. The homemade wine is sweet and powerful. It tastes of autumn's chill, of bright berries crusted with ice and salt, sweet as honey, bitter as marmalade, and a sharpness like burning leaves. I drink again.

Later, my eyes heavy with wine and smoke and weariness, I push open the door to the narrow room that used to be mine. It's all still here; the boat-bed, the deep window, the ship's lantern on the nail. The rustic bookshelves still hold the art books and trinkets I played with as a child, as if eight-year-old Mina has just reluctantly put them back.

Sinking onto the edge of the bed, I see an object on the shelf above so familiar that my heart gives a lurch. A wooden box, with tarnished brass catches. Gently, I take it down and brush dust from the lid.

'Is it for me?' I asked, staring in wonder at the art kit, with its charcoal and pencils and the little squares of paint.

'Of course.' Davy leaned down. 'I paint and write, your Mum takes photos. It's only fair you should join in, don't you think?'

'What do you say to Davy, Mina?' Mum's hair tickled my face as she hugged me, brown paper and ribbons crinkling under her slippered feet.

'Thank you!'

He laughed. 'Well. What are you going to draw first?'

'Murr!'

There are still loose pages of drawings inside, just as I left them on that grey February morning twenty years ago.

I leaf through them, smiling. No wonder my art teacher at school despaired. They're chaotic, exuberant, exploding from the edges of the page. There are pictures of shells and birds and one of Mum and me by a blue sea, but mostly, there are pictures of Murr.

Murr, leaping high over the waves, her fur fluffy and her green eyes flashing. Murr with her bowl of milk. Murr in a boat. Murr wearing a Santa hat.

'*A week isn't long,*' Davy had said, as I put the drawings away. '*They'll be right here waiting for you when you get back after half-term.*'

But he was wrong. That February was the one when everything changed. I went back to London to see my dad, and never returned to Morgelyn. There were no more cosy nights with Mum, planning our new lives on the island, never another Christmas like the one I spent here. Never another word from Davy. Until it was too late.

Shutting the box, I shove it onto the shelf, sink back onto the bed and pull the musty, knitted blanket over my head, fighting down tears.

I'm almost asleep when a floorboard creaks softly and a soft weight flumps onto the bed, settling against my legs. What was it Davy used to say, when he tucked me in? The Cornish for 'goodnight'?

'*Nos dha*, Murr,' I whisper thickly. '*Nos dha*, Mum.'

Nos dha, *Mina.*

CHAPTER SEVEN

My dreams are filled with music. Not a song played with polished wood and steel, but with bone and sand, chittering limpets and the slow scrape of sea snails. A song of sap rising and the hum of bees in the heather, of the seabird's wing and the whisper of salt drying in the sun. And below it all, so soft it's almost inaudible, a low hum, like a woman singing or a cat purring, long into the night.

When I wake, the sound doesn't fade. Instead, it seems to echo through my bones. I open my eyes.

Murr is stretched full on my chest, her eyes half-closed, rumbling deeply.

'Cat,' I protest. 'You're heavy.'

Murr only flexes a paw, digging her claws into the soft woollen blanket.

Slowly, I raise a hand and touch her head. At first I think she'll leap away, but when I smooth her soft ears, she just flexes the other paw, and closes her eyes.

Gently, I stroke that soft fur, my heart swelling, until – as abruptly as if someone has rung a bell – Murr raises her head and leaps down, padding out of the door. A series of loud meows echoes from the direction of the kitchen.

'All right,' I mutter groggily.

The fire has gone out, and the cottage is freezing. Wrapping myself in the blanket, I tiptoe across the icy flagstones towards the little bathroom, with its threadbare, crispy towels. Somehow it feels even colder. How does an old man like Davy cope alone here?

Murr twines around my bare legs as I emerge into the kitchen, meowing insistently.

'I know, I know. I'm hungry too.'

I open a cupboard. The shelves are almost empty, some of the tins at the back rimed with dust and cobwebs. But nearer the front there are newer jars with fancy labels.

'Potted shrimp,' I read, picking one up. 'Is this for you?'

Murr lets out a long and very effusive meow that only grows louder when I twist off the lid and a powerful fishy smell wafts out. 'Ugh, rather you than me,' I tell her, dumping the contents into a bowl. Murr starts purring even before I put it down.

As she snacks happily, I poke around the other shelves. On one, I find half a packet of shortbread biscuits, and on another . . . I take down the jar of gorse blossom honey and crack it open. The smell is just as I remember; sweet as vanilla, musky as dried flowers.

I eat my breakfast of biscuits and honey and tea at the table overlooking the bay, cold feet tucked beneath me. Yesterday's blue sky has vanished; plum-coloured clouds boil over the horizon and the sea is grey as glass, white-capped waves hurling themselves against the rocks. Rain falls softly on the sand and I try to imagine how this day could be, spent slowly wandering the cottage, tidying and pottering around, making tea with the whistling kettle, reading beside the fire as Murr dozes in a fluffy heap on the rug.

But, of course, it can't be like that. I should have used the time last night productively, preparing for my meeting with Jeremy Hunter-Thorpe, looking through the campaign figures I have saved on my phone, making notes to send when I have a signal. It all seems a million miles away, but tonight I'll be back in London and tomorrow Marianne will want briefing on the strategy I'm going to present and what will I tell her when it's not ready? *Sorry, I spent the weekend talking to a cat.*

Sighing, I unlock my phone, silent all night for lack of signal. I might be able to get an hour of work in before I have to leave.

Just as I open up my emails and start to trawl for the ones I need, it starts buzzing with notifications, catching a bar or two of reception. I swipe through them, expecting messages from Paola, and instead see missed calls from my father.

My stomach drops. After years of long silences during my art studies, we're back on speaking terms, though our conversations are usually brief and coolly civil, kept to bland topics like work and weather. And once a month, we go for a Sunday breakfast: a strange, awkward ritual I'm sure neither of us enjoys, feigning casual chat while Julia sits poised to act as referee between us.

Today is Sunday. I stare at the phone for a while, tempted to ignore it entirely. But that might undo the years of careful patching that holds together my relationship with my one surviving parent. With a sigh, I step outside.

Wet, cold sand clogs around my bare feet as I take a few steps up the dunes, searching for a signal. When it picks up half a bar, I brace myself, and call him back.

'Mina,' my father's voice crackles down the line. In the background, I can hear the chatter of the usual chic London café we visit. 'Where are you? I've called three times.'

'Sorry, I can't make it today. Forgot to tell you.'

'Why? Are you ill?'

It would be so easy to lie, to say *yes, not feeling well, so sorry.*

But part of me rebels; wanting to tell the truth even if it hurts. Perhaps *because* it will.

'No.' I clear my throat. 'I'm away. In Cornwall. The Isles of Scilly.'

There's a long silence. When he speaks, there's an edge to his voice. 'What the hell are you doing there?'

'It's Davy. He's ill, in hospital. So I came.'

It sounds so simple said that way, like neat embroidery, not the tangled mess of threads it is.

'What?' He's incredulous. 'How? How did you even know?'

'He sent me a letter, sort of. Julia forwarded it.'

'She . . .?' He makes a strangled sort of noise and I know he's staring at my stepmother furiously across the table. 'Why didn't you tell me? If I'd known you were thinking of going I'd have bloody well stopped you.'

'*How* would you have stopped me? I'm not a kid. I came because I thought it was the right thing to do.'

'Well, it wasn't. You don't owe him anything, Mina. Come home, right now.'

'I'll come home when I'm ready to,' I snap. 'He named me guardian of his estate. The least I can do is make sure—'

'He did *what*?' My father's voice cracks, not just with rage, but with a strange tone I can't decipher. 'How dare he, that old bastard. After everything he did . . .'

He stops. We never talk about Mum, but I know what he's thinking; that Davy was the one who persuaded her to move away from London, taking me with her. That Davy might have even been the one who convinced her to end the marriage and leave Dad in the first place.

He breathes heavily and I know he's fighting to keep himself from yelling. When he speaks again his voice is tight, biting off every word. 'Listen to me, Mina. You know what happened last time that man interfered in our lives. Penhallow doesn't care about you. He never did. He's a selfish narcissist, he's only doing this because he wants something, manipulating you, just like he manipulated your mother.'

'Well, he isn't even conscious,' I say bitterly. Abruptly, my throat constricts. 'And there's every chance he might die, you'll be pleased to know.'

'Mina . . .'

There's something in my dad's voice that sounds almost like desperation, but I can't stay on the phone another moment, hearing my own fears reflected back at me.

'I have to go,' I mutter, and jam my finger to the phone so hard it hurts.

Slowly, I trudge back into the cottage, shivering from more than the chill rain and sea spray. Murr blinks at me from the hearth, with her knowing green eyes.

'Is that true?' I ask thickly. 'Any of it?'

With a huff, she leaps down from the chair and stalks past me out of the front door as if offended. I watch her disappear into the gorse and take a deep breath of the rain-filled sea air.

He's manipulating you, just like he manipulated your mother.

That's what Dad has always believed. Who's to say he's wrong? I was just a child, and my memories here are of the happy times; magical stories and tall tales, riding on Davy's shoulders, his callused hands wrapped in wool as we played cat's cradle. But I remember too the frequent fights between my parents, my mother crying, the feverishness in her voice that day as she told me to pack up a suitcase, that I wouldn't be going back to my old school after the Christmas holidays . . .

I close my eyes, wishing I could go back through time and watch what had actually happened, ask my mum what made her take the leap and finally leave my father, leave behind our life in

London for a new start on these far-flung islands. But she's gone, her parents too, and the only people who can tell me the story are my father or Davy himself.

Did I ever tell you, Mina ...

I cut off the memory of Davy's voice, and the way he always started his stories. Words. Just words. Aren't we supposed to judge people by their actions? All those tales, and yet he never sent even one letter, *one* card when I needed him most. Tangled up in conflicting emotions, I stride to the front door and close it with a snap. Time to leave. I couldn't concentrate on work here even if I wanted to.

Before I go, I venture into the one place I haven't explored. Davy's room looks the same; paintings propped against the walls, the alcove wardrobe covered in a curtain made from painted sail-cloth. When I lift it aside, the smell transports me back twenty years, to hiding in the dark space during a game of sardines, the scent of cedar and dust and old leather and sea lavender tickling my nose as I clung to Murr and tried not to giggle as she settled down grumpily upon the piles of shoes.

I only ever remember Davy wearing fishermen's jumpers and overalls, maybe a paint-stained kerchief knotted at his neck, but now I see that the alcove is full of clothes, many from another time. A fine linen suit, a straw hat, a huge sailor's coat, stained with brine. I hear a whisper of silk, hear the click of glass beads on what must be an evening gown. I don't remember Davy ever mentioning a wife or partner. *You old bachelor*, my mum would always tease.

After a moment's hesitation, I reach up to the shelf. Here are the clothes I remember; heavy woollen jumpers, most of them paint-stained and patched at the elbows but made from good wool, to keep out the cold Atlantic wind.

I pull one down. It feels thick and warm, and abruptly, I realise how cold I am in the stupid silk dress. Quickly, before I change my mind, I drag it over my head. Surely, he wouldn't mind?

Take whatever you like, my father had told me, staring into my mother's wardrobe, his face slack with grief.

Swallowing hard, I grab Davy's dressing gown from the hook, bundling it up with a few pairs of socks to take to the hospital. They'll have to do. I slip out of the room, pulling the door closed behind me.

This time, when I leave, I fill Murr's bowl on the step with milk and place another one of potted shrimp beside it.

'Murr?' I call into the rain-filled morning. 'I'm going.'

There's no answer. She isn't in the bedrooms, or by the hearth, or in the kitchen. Something in my chest squeezes at not being able to say goodbye to her.

'Don't be stupid,' I mutter, as I lock the door.

Though the rain is fine, I'm soon soaked through and shivering hard, thanks to my bare legs and bare head. I look back. In the grey morning light, the cottage looks older than ever, somehow fragile.

'I'm sorry,' I whisper, without knowing why.

By the time I reach the pub, my teeth are chattering and all I want is to be inside, in the warm, not out on the waves. I try the pub's door, hoping for a cup of coffee, but find it locked.

'Great.' Wrapping my arms around myself I hurry over to the shop, only to find that closed up tight too. In fact, the whole island looks deserted. So much for leaving the key with anyone. What the hell is going on? At last I see movement along the beach, a figure in a worn yellow jacket, walking slowly along the shore. I hurry over, slipping and sliding on the pebbles.

'Excuse me!'

The figure stops and turns around. Blue eyes peer out from beneath the hood, bright as the sky reflected in a rock pool. An old man, his face as wrinkled as a walnut, white hair wisping around his face.

'Morning,' I call, catching my breath.

He nods. '*Myttin da.*'

'I don't suppose you know where Gryff, the landlord of the pub is? I need to get over to St Mary's.'

'St Mary's,' he says dreamily, turning his eyes towards the sea. 'Time was we'd walk. Walk the mountain roads that are now just sand.' He looks back to me, sorrow creasing his lined mouth. 'We are losing her.'

'Sorry?'

'Lanbenglas.' He nods across the headland, towards Davy's cottage. 'She's where the gorse grows.'

A shiver runs down my neck that has nothing to do with the cold rain. Just as I open my mouth to ask what he means, the wind changes, bringing the roar of an engine, the whiff of petrol. A sleek white speedboat zooms into the cove, carving a path through the waves before coming to a stop beside the quay. Whoever is driving the boat stands and waves towards me.

I glance back at the old man, but he doesn't respond, only stares sightlessly, his face sad.

Shaking my head, I walk away. As I get closer to the quay, I see it is a woman, in her early forties, perhaps, with rain-swept blonde hair, tasteful gold earrings and a tanned face.

'Don't suppose you're Mina?' she calls up, her accent crisp as cold wine.

How do you know? I almost ask before remembering where I am, how fast news must travel. I shove back the wet hair that clings to my face. 'Yes. Did Gryff send you?'

She raises an eyebrow. 'Gryff from the pub? No, I came out here to look for you, actually. We were expecting you in town last night.' She smiles, showing perfect white teeth. 'I'm Olivia Penhallow.'

'Penhallow?' The name makes me blink. 'Are you related to Davy?'

'That's right. He's my cousin, once removed.'

I stare down at her. I had no idea that Davy had family nearby. And what did Leticia say when I asked? *None he sees eye to eye with.*

'Sorry,' I say stiffly, bracing myself for yet another chilly encounter. 'If I'd known I would have called you.'

She waves a hand. 'Please, it's us who should have called. Look, I came to run you back to St Mary's. Shall we go? You're getting rather wet.'

I glance over my shoulder at the island, and for a moment, think I see a little shape on the headland, grey fur buffeted by the wind ... But it's only a squall of rain across the heather.

'Yes, thanks.'

Swiping my eyes, I climb down the slippery ladder and drop into the boat's pristine interior.

'Gosh,' Olivia says, glancing across from the wheel, 'you've got bare legs. Don't let the palm trees fool you, this isn't the Riviera.'

Before I can explain, she's starting the boat. 'There's a water-proof behind you, put that on.'

Despite my embarrassment, I'm too cold to protest, and huddle the coat over my bare knees, thankful for the fleecy lining as we shoot across the waves in a rush of freezing spray. It's too loud to talk, so I surreptitiously study the woman before me instead. She looks poised, in a way my father might call 'outdoorsy'. In the low winter light, her face looks rather hard, with a long nose and planed cheeks, until she smiles. Then, her eyes crease and I catch a glimmer of a resemblance to Davy, his knowing grin.

In Olivia Penhallow's speedboat, the journey across the water is over in what seems like a flash.

'Must say, I'm awfully glad I ran into you on the quay,' she says as we slow, cruising into the harbour of St Mary's. 'Didn't much fancy trekking all the way across to that creepy old place.' She glances back at me. 'Did you really spend the night there?'

I grimace, a little. 'Not through choice. The pub said they had no rooms and I couldn't find anyone to bring me back.'

She lets out a frustrated sigh. 'Of course. I'm sorry they weren't more helpful. They're a cliquey lot. If they'd called *me* I would have come over and got you in a flash. You could have stayed at the house, we've acres of room.'

'I definitely would've taken you up on that,' I smile. So far, she doesn't seem bothered by my presence. 'But it was fine, actually. I was so tired I just passed out. And Murr kept me company.'

'The cat?' Olivia asks, a little sharply, I think, but maybe it's just the noise of the engine.

'Yes. I fed her this morning so she should be all right for a while.'

Olivia nods. 'You're flying back today, yes?'

'I have to. I only meant to come and check on Davy, return the key. I wasn't expecting any of this—'

'Hungry?' she interrupts, guiding the speedboat through the water like a sharpened blade. 'How about coming up to the house to get dry, have some brunch? Flight's not for a few hours yet.'

I hesitate. I'd planned to get a coffee, do some work while waiting for my flight. And I barely know this woman, after all. What if this politeness is just a façade and she thinks I'm a usurper, barging my way into her family business?

'My sister's there too,' she continues. 'I know she'd like to meet you.'

The thought of spending the entire day in sodden clothes is what sways me. And as soon as I decide, part of me sighs with relief at there being a plan, a sensible, ordinary plan. But only part of me. I take one last look back at Morgelyn, now just a misty smudge on the horizon.

'Thanks,' I tell Olivia. 'I'd like that.'

CHAPTER EIGHT

When Olivia said 'house', I didn't realise she meant House. The building stands on the hill above the town, solid and grey and imposing, with thick hedges that screen it from other properties. Two miniature Christmas trees twinkle with lights on either side of the front door. PENHALLOW HOUSE, a tasteful sign reads.

'You live *here*?' I ask, following her through the high, white gate.

She snorts. 'No, no, we're on the mainland most of the time. This is for holidays. Though it's just Sam and me for Christmas this year. Pa's in Singapore, Mother's decided to jet off to Italy with her new chap, and Sam ...' She glances at me, shakes her head. 'Well, doesn't matter.'

As we walk up the steps, a very elderly bulldog wearing a tartan coat comes plodding out of a fancy dog kennel beside the door. 'Hello, Philip old chap,' Olivia says.

I bend to stroke the dog's head, only for him to sniff me and look up in something like alarm.

'Don't mind him,' Olivia laughs. 'He's going senile. Come in, come in.'

The hallway is immaculate, with a parquet floor and thick cream rugs. It smells of lilies and fresh coffee.

'Sam!' Olivia bellows, shucking off her jacket. 'Visitor!'

I hand back the waterproof, feeling scruffier than ever in my ruined heels and sand spattered legs and Davy's old jumper, even more so when a woman appears at the top of the stairs. She's a few years younger than her sister, and although she shares the same dark blonde hair and grey eyes, her face is softer, rounder. Even on a Sunday morning, she looks as elegant as a model.

'Hello,' she smiles. 'Who are you?'

'This is Mina,' Olivia answers. 'Davy's goddaughter.'

Is it me, or does she put particular emphasis on that title?

'No, really?' Sam's eyes are wide as she pads down the stairs. 'But it's wonderful to meet you! We heard you were on the island.'

She holds my shoulders, bumping her cheek to both of mine, and for a moment I'm engulfed in expensive perfume and the smell of fresh shampoo.

'I'm sorry I didn't call,' I stumble. 'I had no idea Davy had relatives here. He never mentioned you.'

'No, he wouldn't have.' Sam smiles wryly.

'Davy and our mother are like chalk and cheese,' Olivia explains. 'Penhallow and Penhallow never so different.' She claps her hands, making the elderly dog jump. 'Who's for coffee?'

I take off my high heels before walking on that pristine floor. 'Sorry,' I mutter, scrunching my toes. 'I came straight from a party in London on Friday when I heard about Davy. Didn't have time to bring anything.'

'You poor thing,' Sam says, taking my arm. 'Come with me. We'll find you something warmer. And you can have a shower if you like while Livvy makes us food.'

'Charming!' Olivia calls from the kitchen.

Smiling, I let myself be pulled up the thickly carpeted stairs. The rest of the house is just as beautiful as the hallway. Wreaths of fresh holly and ivy have been wound about the stairs, so that the whole place smells like a posh florist's. Crystal decorations hang in the windows, huge poinsettias adorn side tables and windowsills.

'It's a bit OTT, I know, but I adore it here at Christmas.' Sam smiles sheepishly, when she sees me looking. 'Truth be told, I adore it any time of year.'

'But you don't live here?' I ask, as she ushers me into a large bedroom.

'Oh, *I* would in a heartbeat, but they wouldn't like it, you know, Mum or Liv . . .' A look of sadness creases her face before she takes a breath, pushing whatever it was away. She flings open the doors of a built-in wardrobe. 'Right. Let's see.'

Half an hour later I'm freshly showered, smelling of expensive bath products, wearing a soft red cashmere dress and new tights. Olivia grins when she sees me. 'Better?'

'Much. Thanks.'

The huge kitchen windows look out over the bay, a stunning view, all tin-silver sea and bruised grey clouds. A table is laden with a fresh pot of coffee, orange juice, crusty bread, croissants and jam and yellow butter.

'What have the doctors said, about Davy?' I ask, as we eat. 'Have you heard anything more?'

'Not since yesterday,' Sam says, feeding a bit of croissant to Philip. 'They're saying it was quite a serious stroke. From the looks of the scans he'd suffered a few smaller ones over the last couple of months.'

'I doubt he'll be able to go back to the cottage,' Olivia puts in. 'It's hardly suitable for an old man, even one without medical issues.' She catches my expression. 'Listen to us going on. I'm so sorry, Mina. This really isn't anything for *you* to worry about.'

I nod, relief and guilt washing through me in equal measure. 'Thank you. I know Davy wanted me to be guardian, but I have a life in London. I'll do what I can, obviously, but I can't just drop everything.'

'Of *course* not. No one would expect you to.' Olivia pats my hand. 'We'll look after Davy.'

'And Murr?'

A frown flickers across her face, but it's gone in an instant. 'Of course. We can look after the beast until after Christmas. Pop over and look in, feed her, what not.'

'Thank you. I'd really appreciate it. Just until Davy's better, or . . .'

Sam smiles kindly. 'It's no problem, Mina.'

For a while, talk turns to other subjects. Sam is an interior designer and Olivia looks after the family's estate. 'Passed on to me a few years ago,' she says. 'We have the farm on the mainland, and tenanted properties all across the islands. Ma let it go, to be honest, but I'm turning things around.'

'What about your family, Mina?' Sam asks. 'How did they know Davy?'

The question throws me, but there's nothing cruel in Sam's expression. 'My mum was a photographer. I think she met Davy on a trip she took here with some other artists, and they just hit it off. So she asked him to be my godfather, even though my dad never liked Davy. Chalk and cheese, like you said.' I pick up my coffee. 'But Mum loved the islands. We were actually going to move here, when I was a kid.'

'What happened?' Olivia asks. 'Your father said no?'

I shake my head. 'Mum and I came here for Christmas when their marriage broke down, and then stayed for a few months after that.' I look down into the coffee. 'She died, in a car accident, before we got settled.'

Sam reaches out to squeeze my arm. 'Oh Mina, I'm so sorry.'

I give her a reassuring smile, despite the ache in my chest. 'It's all right. All a long time ago.'

Too soon we're finished. I try to help them clear up, but Sam waves me away, so I wander into the hallway instead, looking at the pictures on the walls. Some are landscape photographs, far more prim and proper than my mother's ever were, one or two are professional-looking portraits of a woman with a terrible perm and expensive jewellery, one a much older photo of a group of people in fancy dress, masks in hand. I turn, and in a dark corner beneath the stairs, another portrait catches my eye. This one's a photo of a young man, barely in his twenties, dressed in a Second World War uniform. He has fair hair just like Olivia and Sam's, a proud jaw.

Roaring fills my ears, my eyes blur as if I've stood up too fast.

Candlelight plays across his face as he extends a hand. Her fingers meet his, twining together like seaweed. Water and granite, thorn and blossom . . .

I blink and realise Olivia is standing beside me, asking whether I'm OK.

'Fine, fine,' I hurry, before nodding up at the photo. 'Who's that?'

'That?' Olivia squints up. 'That's Great Uncle George. Handsome devil, wasn't he?'

'He seems so familiar.'

'Not surprised, he was Davy's father.'

'*Him?*'

'Yep. That's why he's stuck in that dark corner. Married low, disgraced the family. His younger brother Edwin, my grandfather, inherited the lot.'

I return the young man's distant gaze. For a heartbeat, I think I hear the crash of waves, smell woodsmoke on winter air, taste apples on my lips so sweet they almost burn . . .

'Mina?' Olivia calls from another room.

Blinking hard, I follow, stepping into a study, with tall

shelves of books that smell of ageing leather and thick rugs and a picture window with a view of the islands. For a second I stand, taking it all in, staring at the patch of cloud and fog that obscures Morgelyn.

'Excuse the mess,' Olivia says, gesturing at a big oak desk covered in papers. 'Listen, Mina, while you're here, I just thought I'd put something to you.' She perches on the edge of the desk. 'Since you have to go back to London, I was wondering if you wanted to pass the guardianship of Davy's estate on to me. I mean, we already administrate properties on the island, so it would hardly be a burden. We'd look after it in exactly the same way we do any other house.'

Heat floods my cheeks. I'm not prepared for this. 'Thanks,' I stammer. 'I'm not sure . . .'

'It would all be perfectly legal. I've already applied for power of attorney as Davy's next of kin. Just thought it might be a way to keep things in the family. And free you up from having to worry about it.'

I pull a smile onto my face. 'Thank you. I'll have to have a think. Maybe talk to Leticia. Is that OK?'

Olivia smiles breezily. 'Of course. Just thought I'd float it. Right, shall I give you a lift to the hospital?'

The photo of Davy's father and the proposition Olivia made linger in my mind as we drive to the hospital in her Range Rover, and walk through the quiet, disinfectant-smelling wards into Davy's room.

Part of me expects him to be awake, to smile and say my name, his eyes full of questions. But he doesn't look any different from yesterday, his eyes closed, his face sagging and blank. I stare at his features, thinking of the young man in the photograph. It seems incomprehensible to me that Davy came from the same family as the wealthy Penhallows. Davy, with his love of peace and anything made by hand, his endless folktales, his cottage, where every chipped flagstone and scrape and scratch has its own story.

While Olivia goes to look for the doctor, and Sam to fetch tea, I sit and start to tell Davy about my day and night at the cottage. About the honey and the seaberry wine, about Murr and the potted shrimp and the milk for the sea spirits, the holly above the door, my dream about an old song … Once or twice I think I see his lips twitch in the ghost of a smile; but I'm probably just imagining it.

'Davy,' I whisper, leaning closer. 'Why didn't you write to me before? I needed this place. I needed you—'

The squeak of the door opening cuts me off. I sit back hurriedly, ready to smile at Olivia or Sam, only to see a tall figure standing there instead, holding a bunch of wildflowers.

It's Jem Fletcher.

'What are you doing here?' he demands.

The bouquet in his hands is made from heather and gorse, wild thyme and sea holly, filling the sterile air with the scent of the shore.

I raise my chin. 'Visiting my godfather. Is that a problem?'

He frowns, but doesn't reply straight away. When he speaks, it's to the far wall. 'Leave the key when you go. I'll look after Murr until Davy's better.'

'Thanks so much,' I reply sarcastically. 'But it's all sorted. Olivia says she'll take care of her. And of Davy.'

'Olivia?' Fletcher's face darkens in a frown. 'Olivia *Penhallow*?'

'Of course. She's family, isn't she?'

Footsteps approach and Sam steps into the doorway, three cups of vending-machine tea balanced in her hands.

'They didn't have—' She stops, pink flushing high on her cheeks. 'Jem.'

A moment later, Olivia appears, looking far less friendly than her sister. 'What do you want, Fletcher?' she barks.

Jem's eyes flick from me, in my borrowed clothes, to the Penhallow siblings and he lets out a bitter laugh.

'What's funny?' Olivia asks.

'You lot. Have you argued over it yet? How much you'll each get when he dies?'

My hand tightens on the bed rail. This again. 'I *only* came to see how Davy is. I came because he asked me to. Because I wanted to help.'

'Yeah, help divvy up the spoils before he's even in the ground.' Olivia laughs scornfully. 'Rich, coming from you.'

'Stop it,' Sam says, her eyes wide. 'Please. For all we know he can hear us.'

'Good,' Jem spits. 'I hope he can.'

He casts one look at Davy, before pushing past Olivia and marching away down the hall.

'What's his problem?' I burst out. 'He was exactly the same yesterday at the cottage.'

'He was there?' Olivia asks.

'Yes. He *said* he came to feed Murr.'

She snorts. 'Probably seeing what he could steal while it was empty.'

'Livvy,' Sam murmurs unhappily.

'Don't defend him, Sam.' She looks back at me, lips tight. 'The man's a criminal, Mina. And he's been sponging off Davy for years. You shouldn't believe a word he says.'

I close my eyes, remembering the file in Jem's hands as he tried to break in through a window, the way he knew his way around the cottage. A tangled web of island politics that I can't even begin to unravel.

'Mina?' Sam touches my arm. 'Don't worry. Anyway, the weather's not looking great. I think we should get you to the airport.'

Nodding, I hesitate before touching Davy's hand. 'Wake up soon,' I tell him. 'Murr misses you.'

His eyes flicker beneath his lids, but nothing more. With a last look, I follow Olivia out. As we step through the hospital doors, a gust of rain-filled wind howls into our faces.

'Did you check the forecast this morning?' she asks, pulling up her collar as we race for the car.

'No. Should I have done?'

'Never know out here.'

By the time we reach the little airport, the rain is coming down hard in great, freezing drops. Inside the terminal building the sound is almost deafening, but out on the runway, I see the tiny propeller plane and a figure that looks like Lou bustling around the wheels. Breathless, I turn to the Penhallows.

'You'll call me?' I ask.

Sam gives me a hug. 'The minute anything changes, yes.'

'The dress . . .' I remember.

'Keep it,' she laughs. 'A gift from Scilly.'

Olivia shakes my hand. 'I'll give you a bell, next time I'm in London.'

The idea seems vaguely absurd, but I smile. 'Great.'

Letting go, I take out the key to Davy's cottage.

'Miss Kestle!' A raincoated figure bursts through the airport doors. It's Leticia Strout, her hair wild. 'You're leaving?' she asks.

'I'm afraid I have to. But it's all right, Olivia and Sam are going to look after Murr until Davy . . . until we know what's happening.'

Olivia grins. 'You can count on us, Tish.'

Leticia doesn't reply, only looks from Olivia to me and back again. 'You can't,' she says at last.

'Can't what?'

'Leave. The weather's too bad. No one will fly in this.'

'They've flown in worse,' Olivia scoffs. 'Look, here's the pilot now.'

Lou pushes her way through the doors, water cascading from her hood. 'Storm's coming in. But if we leave now—' she stops, looking around at us.

'I was just telling them it's too bad to fly,' Leticia says loudly.

Lou gapes for a minute and clears her throat. 'Yes. That's right. Far too bad. Terrible, in fact.'

'You were just about to leave,' Olivia accuses.

'Nope, I was about to say if we leave now we'll be in trouble.' She shrugs at me, with a slightly maddening smile. 'Sorry, Miss Kestle.'

I narrow my eyes at her. This is just like yesterday, at the pub. 'And do you know *when* we'll be able to leave?'

'Not till the storm's blown over.'

'And when might that be?'

She puffs out her cheeks. 'Tonight, tomorrow – who knows?'

'But I have to get back to London! I have work tomorrow.'

'Tell that to the weather, I'm sure it'll listen.'

Right on time, a gust of wind howls against the side of the building, sending the sign rattling.

'It does seem rather foul out there,' Sam says uncertainly. 'Maybe you should stay with us, Mina.'

'Right,' her sister says quickly. 'That way you'll be near the airport, so you can leave as soon as it's clear.'

But something is prickling at the back of my mind, as if the threads that tie me to Morgelyn are being tugged sharply. I look down at the key that's still in my hand.

'Murr,' I say.

'What?' Olivia frowns.

I turn to Leticia. 'Murr was outside when I left this morning. She won't be able to get back in.'

'Gale force winds due, apparently,' Lou says helpfully, scrolling through her phone.

Olivia lets out a snort. 'Mina, it's a *cat*, it'll be fine.'

Leticia steps forward to take my arm. 'I just saw young Lucas Blythe down by the quay, about to head back to Morgelyn. If you hurry, you might be able to catch him.'

For a heartbeat, I look from the Penhallows, to Lou, to Leticia. Then the wind shrieks, the rain batters, and the string around my heart gives a tug so hard I almost cry out.

'Thanks for the food!' I call over my shoulder as I hurry out the door. 'And the clothes. I'll call you later!'

'Mina!' Olivia yells, but within seconds her voice is lost to the sheeting water. Leticia puffs alongside me and we dive into her car.

'Poor Murr,' I gasp, dripping onto the seat. 'She'll be wet through.'

'Don't worry, Miss Kestle,' Leticia says, jamming her foot to the accelerator. 'This isn't the first storm I've raced.'

The little car takes off in a flurry of spray. The rain grows harder with every passing minute, until I can barely see through the windscreen, but Leticia drives like a pro, squinting hard until finally she skids to a halt at the edge of the quay, honking her horn.

'There he is!' she yells. A tiny fishing boat is rising and falling on angry waves.

I stumble out of the car and run down the slippery jetty. 'Morgelyn?' I yell down to the astonished young man in the boat. He peers up at Leticia, who's frantically waving her arms, before holding up his hand to help me aboard.

A minute later, I slip from the ladder onto the crowded deck, packed with nets and lobster pots and plastic crates. 'Hold on,' the young man says, ushering me into the tiny wheelhouse. 'We're in for a bumpy one.'

All of Davy's stories seem true as the boat sets off, ploughing its way across the waves. The sea no longer seems inanimate, a lifeless body of water. Instead it's a beast, hide rippling with life, claws made of foam and salt swiping at the boat like a toy, sending it wallowing from side to side until I'm convinced we're going to go under. I hang on, crammed beside the young man, my stomach churning with the movement, my hands soaked and freezing, and yet, something in me rises in response to all that fury, the sheer ferocity and power. As we're hefted high on the crest of a wave, I find myself laughing. The young man next to me lets out a laugh of his own.

'Wild, right?' A moment later he points through the glass. 'Look, there's Morgelyn, you can see the lights of the Helm!'

I can; an orange glow almost drowned in driving rain. Expertly, the young man brings us into the comparative shelter of the harbour, though the wind still howls and the rain still drives. It's all he can do to hold the boat steady while I grab at the ladder of the jetty. One minute my feet are on the deck, the next the boat has dropped away, four feet below me.

'Thank you!' I yell down, and he gives me a wave before wallowing off towards a mooring.

I swipe water out of my eyes to see a figure waiting for me on the shore, swamped in a huge sou'wester.

'Miss Kestle!' It's Gryff, his face creased with relief. 'You made it. Come in to the pub, come and dry off.'

'I can't,' I call over the weather. 'I've got to find Murr!'

Without a look back I race for the path over the headland, into the maze of gorse. The wind shrieks into my face, chilling my eyes and ears until I'm dizzy with it, barely able to stand, but at last, I stumble down into the cove.

Here, the storm rages, vast explosions of spray arching ten feet in the air as the waves crash against the rocks. Fumbling with the key, I open the door and step inside hoping that – somehow – I might have locked Murr in by mistake.

'Murr?' I shout desperately, before turning to yell into the storm. 'Murr!'

Then, beneath the wind, I hear something: a tiny cry.

Across the cove, a small shape emerges from the gorse and gallops towards me, fur drenched and flattened, racing the storm across the sand. Then, with a wild skittering of paws, she dashes across the threshold and I slam the door closed.

'Murr,' I say, bending down. 'I'm sorry.'

I'm soaked and so is she, fur flat and spiky from the rain. I sit down right there on the floor and haul her onto my lap, trying to rub her dry with my coat, until I'm laughing and she's purring, loud enough to drown out the storm.

CHAPTER NINE

CHAPTER NINE

Did I ever tell you, Mina, the story of how I was made?
'It started with a storm,' I read, as I stroke Murr's head.
'A storm, and a fallen apple.'

The paper crinkles in my hand. It's one of Davy's stories. I found it in the dresser drawer, when I was looking for some paper to scrawl down notes on my presentation to Hunter-Thorpe.

Around me, the cottage glows, the grey evening warmed by oil lamps. A fire burns bright in the grate, as outside the storm howls and rain lashes the panes. I'm snug, in a huge pair of Davy's knitted socks and a jumper, a blanket tucked around me, and a glass of seaberry wine at my elbow. Murr sits in the armchair opposite, fed and full, her bright eyes half-closed in contentment.

Leticia promised to let me know as soon as flights are given the all clear. I feel a stab of anxiety about the fact that the day is waning, that it's now almost impossible I'll make it back to London in time for work tomorrow, but really, it's out of my hands. I've already managed to send Marianne a grovelling email about a family emergency, promising that I'm working on the presentation for Wednesday and will fill her in as soon as I can, and another to Paola explaining the situation. There's not much more I can do.

'Shall I read the rest?' I ask.

With a great yawn, Murr stretches out one fluffy paw as if to say *go on*.

I smile. What's the harm? It won't take long, and then I can get back down to work. 'They were winter apples,' I continue, hearing Davy's voice in every comma, every word. 'Ruddy-cheeked as if they had spent too long in front of a fire, so sweet they almost burned the tongue. And the basket belonged to a beautiful girl who was like the winter herself.'

Her hair was black as a guillemot's wing and her eyes were golden as the low December sun and her skin was pale brown as winter heather. She wasn't alone: she walked with her cat, who was grey as smoke, soft as ash.

It was a Sunday. And for most that meant the sailor's chapel, and for others it meant collecting winkles, and for fewer still it meant killing for sport, prowling with guns and liquor, chasing the rabbits that the servants set loose upon the island they saw as theirs.

One man in particular went creeping through the heather, his gun ready. And when he spotted a whisk of grey through the furze, he fired – though secretly he hated to – his gun cracking with a noise like thunder. In its wake, he heard a woman cry out. Frightened, he stumbled from the furze and found himself on the headland, where a woman stood, a basket of fallen apples at her feet.

And when the man looked at her, he thought he had slipped into the faery realm, because she was as beautiful as the dawn on Midwinter's Day, standing beside a cat with eyes as green as sea glass. And he remembered the old stories of sea maidens and buccas that his nanny had once told him, that his teachers had dismissed as local superstition.

Not knowing what else to do, he picked up an apple and offered it back, but the girl only smiled mockingly and said, 'Go ahead and keep it, sir, don't you own everything else?'

And her scorn caught him like the gorse. He looked at her – in her worn knitted coat and her muddy, patched boots – and he knew he was lost. His hunting friends found him wandering the shore hours later, a half-eaten apple in his hand and a dazed look in his eye. They roused him with taunts and jibes, and got him onto the boat and took him back to the comfort of his grand old house on the big island.

But that was not the end, you see. Because he found he could think of nothing but those eyes like candlelight and the taste of winter apples and her laugh like a thorn. Nothing could distract him, not the brandy decanter, not the brush of silk or the sting of tobacco, not the latest American songs on the gramophone, or the news of the Winter War simmering in the icy north.

And so, on Midwinter's Eve, he went forth with the rest of his jolly party, disguised so none might know them, a lion's mask upon his face and a golden necklace in his pocket with a stone of yellow garnet, the colour of her eyes.

Across the waves, the tiny island where she lived was strung with lights that fizzed and crackled with the newly brought electricity, accordions and pipes and drums filled the air, spiced cider sloshed into cups to toast the longest night. He followed his friends into the dances on the shore like a man in debt to dreams.

And at midnight, when the islanders threw their wreath of sea holly and heather onto the waves, he saw her. She was dressed as a maiden of the sea, in a gown of silken tatters, her hair all loose down her back.

Their eyes met. He extended a hand and her fingers met his, twining together like seaweed. Water and granite, thorn and blossom, he held on, and to his wonder, she drew him to her, into the dance.

And if his friends didn't see him again that night – what of it? On Midwinter's Eve there are no rules. No boundaries or divisions. Only fire in the night, only the voices singing to the sea, only the quickness of hearts, beating in defiance of the dark.

And if the man married his fierce love in a tiny island chapel, if he was turned from the grand house by his family and shunned by his friends for doing so, what of it? He did it in joy. He did it with a sprig of gorse in his lapel, and the taste of winter apples on his tongue and a grey cat as their witness.

He did so with love, lodged like a thorn in his heart.

My sleep is restless, broken by the sounds of the storm raging outside, by the boom of the waves against the rocks. More than once I think I hear voices; cries of alarm, people whispering softly beside the fire, but when I wake enough to listen, I realise it's only Murr. She sits at the porthole window, staring out and making quiet noises, as if conversing with the storm. For some reason, it makes me feel safe, watched over, and I burrow deeper beneath the quilt, falling back into the billows of sleep.

When I wake at last, it's to a sky as dark as twilight. The rain has stopped, but the wind seems even stronger, driving waves against the coast so powerfully I can feel it in my bones. Monday morning, I realise in disbelief. It's Monday morning. I should be running from the Tube, grabbing coffee, dodging Christmas shoppers and instead I'm here, in a weather-beaten cottage, dozens of miles from the nearest office block, where days of the week don't seem to exist.

A strange smile spreads across my face, as if I'm skipping school.

At the table I turn on my phone, down to its last scraps of battery. Scrolling past the handful of demanding messages from my father, I click on Paola's instead.

> Any update?? Don't forget we have to go
> through the H-T account today.

Hello?!

Mina!!!

I type out a quick reply.

> Sorry P!!!

> Still in Cornwall, stuck on the island. Bad
> weather = no flights. Going to try later
> today ...

I hesitate.

> Or tomorrow. Am working here. Will send my
> notes and call Marianne later.

> Cover for me? x

A series of loud yowls from the kitchen tells me that I'm unforgivably late with breakfast.

'All right, your majesty,' I call, balancing the phone on the top of the dresser, where it sometimes manages to find a signal.

I spoon out the final jar of potted shrimp for Murr, share the last drop of milk between us. By the time I carry my tea back to the table, Paola's reply is waiting.

Already covered

Bigged up your family emergency. Marianne
was 😕 and said you HAVE to be back
by tomorrow. Hunter-Thorpe, Wednesday
10.30 a.m.??!!!

I stare at the words. For some reason, my life in London seems unreal. By contrast, everything here is solid, tangible, as if someone has turned the saturation up.

After a second's hesitation, I hold my finger to the power button and watch the screen go dark. I'll turn it on later to call Marianne, once I find somewhere with electricity and a charger. The phone's dark surface reflects my face.

Just water and sky, I remember Mum saying, her eyes closed as she basked in the winter sun. *This place is just what I needed.*

'Well,' I tell Murr. 'If I'm going to be stuck here all day, we'll need provisions.'

She looks up mid-bath, pink tongue sticking out in a way that makes me laugh.

Beside the door, I stick my arms into Davy's huge oilskin coat and cram an old knitted hat over my hair. The pair of wellies I find are almost comically big, but at least my feet will be dry. Bracing myself, I wallow outside, calling goodbye to Murr as I shut the door behind me. As I reach the path, I hear a squeak and turn to see one of the lower windowpanes in Davy's studio swing open, like a flap. Murr emerges and trots towards me, her fur blown about by the gusts of wind.

I stare disbelievingly. 'You had your own door, this whole time?'

She twines around my legs for a moment before galloping off up the path with the wind in her tail.

She accompanies me as far as the headland, where she stops, batting at something that rolls on the sand, chasing it towards my feet. An apple, I realise in surprise. A small winter apple, half-eaten, as if someone dropped it only moments before. But when I look around there's no one, no sign of any footprints but my own.

'Where did you find this?' I turn to ask Murr, but she's gone. Neck prickling, I carry on, down towards the village.

Today, at *last*, the shop is open, Christmas lights twinkling around a window display of puddings and a giant wheel of cheese. The bell over the door jangles merrily to announce my presence. The two older women from the pub stand before the tinsel-festooned counter. The place is so small, it's impossible to ignore them.

'Morning,' I greet awkwardly, taking one of the wicker shopping baskets.

'Morning,' they each reply slowly, staring at me until I step around the shelves. As soon as I'm out of sight, they start whispering.

'She's still here then?'

'Storm brought her back.'

'Is it true, you reckon?'

'Wylym thinks so. Said old Davy knew to call to her, as soon as the gorse came in.'

'And what of Murr?'

The bead curtain behind the counter clatters and another voice calls out. 'Right, that's your turkey ordered, Sue. Now . . .'

They change the subject, talking of other things – the Christmas lights to be put up, whether the pub will be able to hold the troyl or not. Still, their words prickle in my mind, *said old Davy knew to call to her, as soon as the gorse came in . . .* What on earth are they talking about? Shrugging it off, I go back to exploring the shelves.

Tiny as it is, the shop seems to stock everything, and I smile, remembering the fun my mother and I once had, picking out things for our Christmas feast. Biscuits and candied almonds, satsumas and wrinkled walnuts, a bottle of ruby-coloured port and ham glazed with honey and stuck with cloves. Smoked salmon and thick cream for Murr.

Wrapped in fond memories, I look over every shelf until, on one, I find a huge display of potted fish products. Reading the sign, I smile. *GRYFF'S CUISINE*, it says, in curling letters. *HANDMADE ON MORGELYN.*

I drop six jars of the stuff into the basket, alongside a few cleaning supplies, a toothbrush, freshly baked crusty bread and local butter, milk, wine, chocolate, tea, new-laid eggs ... Who knows how long the storm will last, I think, with a sort of cheerful abandon. By the time I heave the basket onto the counter, the two women have gone.

'With you dreckly!' comes a yell from the back room. Looking down at the spiced pastries and baked goods on display, my stomach gives a growl.

'Right,' a woman with grey-black hair and a pair of huge glasses says, wiping her hands. 'What can I ...' She stops when she sees me.

'Morning,' I say brightly. 'I'll take all of this. And two mince pies. And one of those samosas, please. Thanks.'

She nods, smiling a little knowingly. 'You'll be staying a while then, Miss Kestle?'

'Just until the storm blows out.'

'Should have passed by tomorrow.' She rings through some toothpaste, glancing at me beneath her dark lashes. 'Shame you can't stay for the troyl on Wednesday, though.'

'Troyl?'

She nods. 'We always have one on Midwinter's Eve, dress up, have a laugh.'

Torchlight on the waves, spiced cider flowing, hands meeting in a dance.

I drag my attention back to what the woman is saying. '... might be the last one.'

'Sorry? The last what?'

'The last troyl.' She leans forwards across the counter, eyes wide behind the glasses. 'Between you and me, the Helm's in terrible trouble. They've only got a few rooms and the summer visitors just aren't enough to cover the rent and the repairs any more. That and Gryff's latest scheme going belly-up.' She waves one of the jars of shrimp ruefully. 'Although you seem to have taken a liking to it.'

'It's not for me,' I confess. 'It's for Murr.'

The woman chuckles. 'That cat will be fat as a hen in no time. I don't know, Murr eating potted shrimp.' She laughs again, ringing up the items.

'How old is Murr?' I ask, leaning on the counter. 'I can't work it out. There was a cat here with the same name when I was little, but that was twenty years ago.'

'Ooh, now, let me think.' She squints. 'I've been here ten years, and she's been with Davy that whole time.'

'Well, she's either ancient or a different cat.'

She shrugs. 'Must be.'

As I take the laden paper bags, the woman holds up a finger. 'Wait a tick.' She disappears into the back and returns with a little package wrapped in paper. 'A few scraps for Madam Murr. On the house.'

Outside, boats roll dangerously on the vast swells, spray arching high over the edge of the jetty. A couple of children shriek and dance on the shore, deliberately trying to get soaked – school must have been called off. A memory stirs of a primary school on one of the smaller islands, a building with only a handful of pupils compared to my school in London, and a school boat every morning instead of a school bus. *What do you think, Mina?* Mum had asked, on the January morning we'd visited. *Would you like to go to school here?* And I had smiled and told her *yes* because it all felt like an adventure.

With the children's laughter ringing in my ears, I turn away. Another Mina's life.

Outside the Helm, Gryff shelters in the doorway, smoking glumly and staring at something on the patch of lawn before the pub. A moment later he chucks the stub away and stomps back inside.

I can't help myself. Juggling the bags, I wander over to look. A white plastic sign has been driven into the ground.

PROPERTY OF PENHALLOW ESTATES, it reads, in blocky red letters.

Olivia mentioned properties, didn't she? And that the pub was on the verge of being condemned? Sighing, I look up at the dilapidated place. Poor Gryff.

I arrive back at the cottage a sweaty, windswept mess. Unpacking the bags, I open the paper package the shop lady gave me and find not scraps but fresh cuts of fish, good enough to sell. As soon as she hears the rustle, Murr appears as if by magic, letting out a long meow.

'You obviously have admirers,' I tell her.

While she eats enthusiastically, I find an old radio and tune it to a fuzzy station that's playing traditional carols. Belatedly I realise that I forgot to ask in the shop about charging my phone. But it's raining now, and Marianne will be in meetings for the rest of the morning anyway. To the sound of distant voices and soothing fiddle music, I set about cleaning, humming as I go. I only mean to do a little, sweep away the crumbs and distracting cobwebs and dust before finally getting down to some work, but one job becomes another and soon I'm sweating, jumper rolled over my elbows, buffing soot and grime from the windows, dislodging thick dust from the mantelpiece and picture frames. I sweep the flagstone floors and relocate a sleepy heap of cat to the window seat, so I can beat the armchair's cushions, sending years of dust and cat hair swirling into the roaring winds.

I leave Davy's room until last. It feels wrong, to be busying around in here, but Olivia was right about him being an old man. Even if he makes a good recovery he'll hardly be able to clean it himself when he returns. *If he returns*, a little voice says, but I shove it away. I brush the windowsill of dead flies, sweep the floor, dust the headboard, made from a huge chunk of driftwood. Murr appears, intrigued by the comings and goings, and settles down in the middle of the bed as if challenging me to try and move her from *that* spot, too.

'A lot of this dander is yours,' I tell her. 'Don't you ever lend a hand? That tail would make a good duster.'

With a sniff of disdain, she turns away only for her ears to prick up. Her whole posture changes, becoming taut, alert. I yelp as a huge spider scuttles away from my broom, making for the darkness of the wardrobe. Watching it, Murr hunkers down low, her backside wiggling.

'No, Murr, leave it!'

With a great leap she clears the end of the bed and lands on the floor, batting at the spider, all flashing eye and swiping paw. It gets free, darting into the curtain-covered alcove but she pounces after it.

I laugh at the sound of frantic scrabbling, shoes tumbling, hangers clattering, and pull back the curtain to see the carnage. Wild green eyes stare out at me from the darkness of the top shelf, where Murr has somehow managed to climb.

'How did you get up there?' I chide, but as I reach to lift her down, she leaps over my head, landing on the bed with a *flump* and sending a huge hat box tumbling from the shelf in the process. I grab for it, too late. The box hits the floor, spilling its contents all over the rug.

Papers. What look like dozens and dozens of letters.

'Great,' I groan as I bend to pick them up.

There must be nearly a hundred here ... some look like

greetings cards and others like longer missives, folded into fat envelopes. Curiosity pricks at me, even though they're obviously private. I start to scoop them back into the box, only to stop dead when I see the impossible.

My name – my old name – there in black and white.

> Miss Mina Martinovszky
> 8 Orchard Road
> Larrington
> Sussex

My father's house. The place we lived before Mum and I moved to Morgelyn for those two, dream-like months. The place I returned to during holidays from boarding school, after she died. But the address has been crossed through, eight words scrawled on the bottom of the envelope in my father's handwriting.

> RETURN TO SENDER: NO LONGER AT
> THIS ADDRESS

The letter hasn't even been opened. Heart in my throat, I stare, before shakily turning the letter over and breaking the seal. Inside is a hand-drawn Christmas card, showing a stylised cottage in a snowstorm, a cat's silhouette in the candlelit window.

> Dearest Mina,
>   With all our best thoughts on the Yuletide.
>   Your Godfather, Davy
>   And your friend, Murr

There's an inked pawprint on the other face of the card. I

touch it gently before grabbing the envelope. It is postmarked
three years ago. I reach down to sift through the rest of the
letters, pulling out any that are addressed to me. Rage builds in
my chest, merging with sorrow and disbelief, as I find dozens, at
least two a year for twenty years, every Christmas, every May for
my birthday. All of them unopened, all with that same scrawled
rejection, NO LONGER AT THIS ADDRESS, again and again
across the front.

Finally, I see another letter among the pile, different to the
others. It looks businesslike, franked with the name of my father's
company, dated the year my mother died. This one is addressed
to Davy, and has been opened. Swiping at my eyes, I rip it from
the envelope.

Dear Mr Penhallow,

Please desist in your attempts to contact my daughter. She
is in a fragile emotional state, and all your letters do is upset
her further. I wish for her to be able to continue her school-
ing with as little disruption as possible.

There is absolutely no question of her visiting you. It
was Helena's decision to name you godfather; a decision
I agreed to for her sake and against my instincts. You are
not a relative or a friend, and I am not hesitant to say that I
believe you were a bad influence on my ex-wife, and were in
part responsible for both the events and the poor judgement
that led to her death. Furthermore, a visit to the very county
where her mother died would be far too traumatic for Mina.

Consider this my final word on the matter. Any and all
further correspondence will be returned unopened for my
daughter's sake.

Sincerely,

Mr Jonathan Kestle

At once, it all comes flooding back; the loneliness I felt at school, the sadness that Davy never wrote, my father comforting me in his brusque way, saying, *Don't give that man another thought, Mina.* But the hurt I felt all these years – believing that Davy abandoned me – is nothing compared to the desperate sorrow that goes through me now, surrounded by proof that he cared, that he tried and kept trying, proof that I was wrong; that my father had been the one to cause me all that pain, out of bitterness or misplaced concern. Tears burn my eyes and I let out a sob for all the lost years.

'Davy,' I cry. 'I'm so sorry.'

CHAPTER TEN

20 October

Dear Davy,

I hope you are OK and get this letter OK too. The last one must have got lost. I am writing to send you my new adress, the adress is Wickersley Vale School, Fromersham, East Sussex. If you put my name on the envelope I will get it.

I have been here for 1 month now. It's OK. But I wish I was going to the school on Tresco island instead.

Could I visit Morgelyn for Christmas like last year? Dad says it's too far and I shouldn't ask you, but I thought I would ask just in case.

I am sending a toy I made for Murr in craft lesson. It's a fish made of felt and string, and it's blue because that's her favrite colour. If I come for Christmas I can wrap it up for Murr to open on Christmas Day.

Please write back and say if you think it
will be OK?
Lots of love,
Mina (Martinovszky) ×

Dearest Mina,
   Thank you for your letter; I was very happy to hear from you.
I am so sorry that I was not able to see you in March at your
mother's funeral. Please trust that I was there in my thoughts.
   I hope you're happy at your new school, though I know it
must be a big change. As for your letter asking to come for
Christmas; you will always be welcome on Morgelyn. Spring or
winter, snowfall or sunshine, Murr and I will be here waiting.
   I will write to your father and tell him so, if you like.
   With fond memories and fair dreams,
   Your Godfather,
   Davy

My tears fall onto the letter, read for the first time after all these
years. I cry for that grieving eight-year-old girl waiting in vain
for a reply, for a friendly word that would have soothed her
heart. I cry for Davy and the fact this letter was returned to him
unopened, the words: *unable to deliver* printed in my old head-
mistress's neat handwriting, no doubt doing what she thought
was best by following my father's instructions. I cry for all the
time we've lost, and the fact it might be too late.

   Wiping my eyes, I pick up my father's letter to Davy and read
it again, feeling as if I have a lump of iron in my chest. What did
he mean, *responsible for the events and the poor judgement that led
to her death*? How could Davy have had anything to do with a
car crash? I keep reading, and another sentence strikes me cold.

A visit to the very county where her mother died would be far too traumatic for Mina.

I was never sure *where* it happened. On the A30, that was what the adults around me said, just another thing that didn't make sense, in a world where everything had been torn apart. Later, I didn't want to know – couldn't bring myself to ask, because asking would mean imagining it happening.

But what if she had been driving back *here*, after taking me to London to stay with Dad for half term? Questions hurtle through my mind, demands, a thousand *what ifs* . . . Most of all, anger. That the one person who was supposed to love me most lied to me for all these years. Pushing myself to my feet, I grab at my phone and turn it on, knowing it only has 5 per cent battery and not caring. Murr looks up from her cushion by the fire as I wrench open the door and stumble out onto the sand. I press the call button again and again, until finally – on the slope of the dune – I get some signal and it begins to ring.

'Mina?' my father answers. I have to press the phone to my ear to hear him over the sound of the wind and the waves.

'How could you?' the words burst from me, into the buffeting air. 'How could you do this to me, to Davy?'

'What are—'

'I found the letters, Dad. In Davy's house. He wrote to me, he's *always* written and you didn't tell me!' I swipe at my face. 'Why?'

Silence thunders between us, filled by the raging crash of the surf. When my father speaks, he sounds old. 'Penhallow has always been unstable, a jealous man. He would have turned you against me, taken you away like he did your mother.'

'It wasn't for you to decide!'

'You have to understand—'

'No, *you* understand. You stole this from me. This place, everything it meant. And now it might be too late.'

'What was I supposed to do? Let another man, a stranger, bring you up?'

'Well, he might have done a better job than you.'

The words are from my mouth before I can stop them, stinging like salt on raw flesh. For a long moment, I think my father will cry or hang up, but then he speaks again, putting on a voice, the logical, hard-edged one he uses to win arguments.

'It's not real, Mina. What Penhallow peddles, it's a fantasy, not real life. See how he's already come between us without saying a word? How you're already risking your career because of him?' He makes his voice calm. 'Come back and we'll talk about this. Don't do anything rash. Don't throw everything away on a charlatan like Davy Penhallow.'

'I could have had a life here.'

'Your mother thought the same thing and look what happened to her.'

The words are like a slap across the face. As if dying were her fault . . . I can hear my father clear his throat on the other end of the phone, knowing he's gone too far.

'Mina . . .'

My phone dies. I let my hand fall from my head, and the sound of the sea floods into the space where my father's voice was. I breathe it in, the scent of the island filling my nose, sharp winter green, wet sand, seaweed, the distant tang of woodsmoke. Beneath the wind I hear a soft noise and look down. Murr has come to find me. Kneeling, I bury my wet face in her soft, cold-clung fur.

When I sit back, she blinks at me slowly as if to say, *Now do you see?*

Smiling a little, I follow her back into the cottage.

*

A knocking wakes me. I raise my head from my arms, bewildered, only to realise I must have fallen asleep at the table, exhausted after everything that's happened.

'Mina?' a voice calls. 'Are you there?'

Wincing at a crick in my neck, I stumble to open the door.

The wind hits me full in the face, but it feels less powerful now, as if its anger is flagging, reduced to upset squalls rather than one long roar.

In the last grey dregs of daylight, Olivia Penhallow stands, hair windswept, a posh supermarket bag in one hand. A small yacht dances up and down on the waves of the cove, a dinghy pulled onto the shore.

'There was a lull in the storm so I thought I'd zip across, bring you some ...' Her smile falters when she sees my face. 'Mina, what's happened?'

I must look a total state. My nose feels blocked, my eyes hot and sore. 'I'm all right,' I tell her croakily. 'Come in.'

While she unpacks the treats she's bought me – a bunch of lilies 'to brighten up the place', salmon sandwiches, expensive biscuits – I tell her everything; about all the letters I never received, about the terrible phone call with my father that followed.

'I just can't believe he would lie to me for so long,' I say, hurling a teaspoon into the sink.

Olivia picks up another of Davy's Christmas cards, which now lay scattered across the table. 'Why do you think he did it?'

I rub at my eyes. 'I think he blames Davy for the fact my mum left, and for persuading her to come here. If she hadn't, she might still be alive.'

It hurts me to think it, let alone say it, that my bright memories of Morgelyn might have come at such a cost.

'You can't know that,' Olivia says kindly. 'And it doesn't help to speculate.' She peers at another card. 'Must say, I do get where your pa is coming from a little, wanting to keep you safe as a kid. Maybe he thought you'd try to run back here or something.'

'I did.' The memory hits me like a wave. 'I did try to once. The first Christmas after Mum died, I snuck out of the school with fifty pence. I got as far as the bus stop before someone realised where I'd come from and called the school. Dad was furious.'

I sag back in the chair, remembering how my breath had misted in the freezing morning, the headlights of the bus, the way I'd memorised every step of the route: *bus to the station, train to London. Tube to Paddington. Train to Penzance. Walk to the ferry. Ask to go to Morgelyn.*

'And he must have been scared stiff of losing you,' Olivia says pointedly. 'Like I bet he is right now.'

I want to argue, but a small part of me knows she's right. I've never seen my father show much emotion, but I heard it in his voice today.

'If he thinks he's going to get a free pass, that he doesn't have do something to earn—' I stop abruptly, an idea blooming into life.

'What?' Olivia asks, raising an eyebrow.

'You said yourself Davy would struggle here if he gets out of hospital. But what if I can make it so that he doesn't have to struggle? What if I could find him help, make this place work for him?'

'I don't think Davy has that kind of money.'

'No, but my dad does. If he wants to make amends to me, *this* is how he can do it. By making sure Davy can stay in his own home.' I sit back, smiling at her, mind racing.

Olivia doesn't seem convinced. 'We still don't know what will happen with Davy.' Seeing my smile falter, she rallies. 'But in any case, he's jolly lucky to have you as a goddaughter.'

She clinks her mug with mine and I return the smile.

'Got a vase for these?' she asks, nodding to the flowers.

By the time I return with one made from green blown glass, Olivia has her phone out, taking pictures of the cottage. 'For Sam,' she smiles. 'I told her I was coming and she asked for a snap. Neither of us has seen this place in years. Must say, it looks a bit nicer now that you've smartened it up.'

She drops into the armchair, crossing her feet before the fire. She looks so odd sitting there, with her coiffed blonde hair and gilet, so smart and polished in a place where everything is worn and carefully repaired, that I laugh.

'What?' she demands.

'Nothing. Just . . . that's Murr's chair.'

She leaps to her feet and, sure enough, her tight-fitting black jeans are plastered with grey fur. Making a rueful face, she tries to brush herself down. 'Where is the beast, anyhow? I would've thought it would be here, lording it by the fire. Isn't that what cats do?'

'Most of the time, yes.' I glance around but all of Murr's usual spots are empty. 'She must have gone out.'

Olivia laughs. 'Well, please convey my apologies to her ladyship for sitting in her chair.' She glances through the window. 'I'd better be off, before that wind starts up again and my skipper turns apoplectic.'

Outside, night is rapidly falling. Olivia pauses in the doorway, cheerily zipping up her waterproof. 'You're back to London tomorrow?'

I sigh. There's really no putting it off. 'I wish I didn't have to, but there's something I have to do. Dad's right that I should at least *try* to keep my job.'

'Roger that. Pop into the house before you go to say cheerio to Sam, have some Christmas cake.'

'Thanks.'

She nods, waving a hand. 'Until tomorrow, then.'

I wave as she pushes the dinghy out onto the waves and expertly leaps in. Only when I turn away do I spot the shape at the edge of the thicket, shadow against shadow. Murr, her green eyes fixed, silently watching the boat depart.

'Damn.'

Crinkling up the piece of paper, I throw it towards the fire. It lands on the hearthrug where Murr sprawls, luxuriating in the heat. Lazily, she bats at the paper ball before stretching out a paw.

'Stay still,' I tell her.

Several other failed attempts litter the hearth, or have blossomed into flame in the grate. I found the sketchpad and the pencils in Davy's art room, decided there was no harm in giving it a try, even if I am out of practice. As the storm sputters outside, I turn the page and try to concentrate. How long since I stopped buying pens and sketch pads, stopped sending out my portfolio to agencies and agreed, finally, to give up chasing a silly dream and take a sensible job instead? I lower the pencil to the page.

Don't think too much, Davy always said. I remember the day he told me that, in the little studio. Mum sat on an old chair, posed in a fantastical costume, candles glittering around her, ivy wound into her hair. Seeing me looking, she gave a wink.

'Don't try to capture what you see,' Davy said, his sleeves already spotted with green paint. 'Try to capture what you feel.'

Half closing my eyes, I let the pencil hang loose in my hand and start to draw, trying to do what Davy said and focus on a feeling instead of a shape. I send the pencil arching in time with roar of the waves outside, the whistle of wind down the chimney. I bring it back in soft curves; the curl of Murr's paw, the plume of her tail, held aloft as she runs to greet me, the hidden patterns that exist in her grey fur, stripes like the meanderings of sea snails, like currents beneath the water.

Finally, I peek down at what I've drawn, and sigh. It's just a mess of lines. I'm about to crumple it up when shapes begin to show themselves through the chaos. Isn't that an arm, curved protectively, loving, sheltering? Isn't that falling snow, swirling hair, a woman's face? Isn't that the shape of a cat, keeping watch on a long winter's night?

Slowly, I put the pencil aside and slide down to the floor beside Murr, the way I used to as a kid. When I stroke her fur, the storm outside quietens, and abruptly, I realise what Leticia meant when she said she couldn't *take* Murr; no one could. She's as much a part of this place as the gorse and the sand and the stones of the beach. This place is hers, if it is anyone's.

As if she hears my thoughts, Murr stretches a paw upwards to touch my chin, and I hear Davy's voice as clearly as if he sits beside me.

The people who went before are all around us, Mina, if only we could learn to hear them.

'I'm listening,' I whisper.

CHAPTER ELEVEN

I wake to blue skies. Outside it's a glorious winter morning, as if the storm has scoured the world with salt and left it fresh and clean. I open the front door and a lively sea breeze rushes in, snatching away the powerful scent of the lilies Olivia brought, replacing it with the smell of frost on the heather and cold seaweed and wet sand.

Papers stir on the table. Davy's stories and Christmas cards sit alongside the sketches that I sat drawing deep into the night. The cottage, the cove, the rocks and the sea, a girl in swirling snow, Murr standing proud on the headland, facing down a storm with electricity in her tail . . .

Childish, my father would have said, and it's true, they're far from my best work. But I smile as I gather them together and tie them with a scrap of green ribbon from the drawer. On a clean page, I write a note in pencil.

Dear Davy,
    Here are twenty drawings, one for every year we lost.
    Murr says get well, and come back to Morgelyn soon.
All my love, Mina x

My heart aches as I tuck them into my bag to leave with Davy at the hospital. I pack up my few things, wishing absurdly that the storm had kept blowing, day after day, all the way to Christmas. I wish I could stay here, walking down to the cosy pub for mulled wine of an evening, watching the lights of the other islands across the bay, lighting the fire on windswept mornings. But I have to go back. I have a life back in London, a sink full of unwashed dishes, a job, responsibilities that I can't keep putting off for ever, and now – I look out at the streaming sunlight – there's really no excuse.

Murr knows something's up. She follows me around the cottage as I pack, and only eats a little of her potted shrimp. When I return from the bathroom – and another chilly wash with a kettle of hot water – I find her sprawled defiantly across my handbag, claws dug into the fake leather.

'I'll be back,' I tell her, tears in my eyes. 'I promise. In the meantime, Olivia will look after you, and soon Davy will be home.'

She only blinks at me, her bright green eyes duller than usual, and headbutts my arm softly.

'Oh, Murr,' I tell her. 'I *have* to go.'

Gently, I unhook her claws from the bag and pick her up, burying my face in the soft fur that smells of cold air and gorse. Then, before I can stop myself, I settle her in her chair and hurry out of the cottage.

This time, I leave the key behind Murr's bowl, for someone else.

When I reach the path, I half-turn back, my breath misting in the cold air, expecting to hear the cat door swing open, soft paws padding towards me. But there's nothing, just the breeze over the frost-tipped heather, the wash of the waves in the cove, the high, solitary cry of a curlew. I hunch into my jacket and turn away.

The rest of the island, by contrast, seems busy. I wave to the shopkeeper, sweeping away flotsam outside her shop, and see the strange old man I spoke to sunning himself on a bench. Outside the Helm, Gryff stands alongside Elodie and Jem Fletcher, all of them staring grimly at the building and the damage wrought by the storm. The thatch looks in an even worse state than when I first saw it, one eave almost bare. I hesitate, torn between saying goodbye and having to bear another round of scorn from the Fletcher siblings, when Gryff sees me.

'Miss Kestle!' he cries, trying his best to put on a merry smile. 'Survived the storm, eh?'

'Yes, thanks.'

'Where are you off to? Not leaving?'

'Afraid I have to. My boss is already going to kill me. But I'll come back after Christmas, once I've sorted a few things. And in the meantime, Olivia is going to feed Murr, so she should be fine.'

'Olivia?' Elodie asks, unmistakable aversion in her voice.

My shoulders stiffen. 'Yes. Why not?'

But she only makes a disgusted noise and walks away into the pub. Jem says nothing, just stares at me, a slight frown between his brows.

Gryff sighs. 'Sorry about El, Miss Kestle. She's taking the loss of this old place rather hard.'

He stares glumly at the sign in the sandy grass, with its reminder that the pub is owned by Penhallow Estates.

Abruptly, I feel like an idiot. 'I'm sorry, Gryff. I didn't mean . . .'

'It's not your problem, now, is it?' he says kindly, and holds out a big, stove-burned hand.

As I reach to shake it, a stray gust of wind springs out of nowhere, playful as a cat, clawing at my overstuffed bag and whipping my coat and hair. The bundle of drawings I made for Davy goes flying, scattering like leaves across the ground.

Swearing, I try to grab them before they're blown into the water, but the wind is mischievous, batting them away even as I bend to grab them. I hear Gryff's muffled guffaw as a page slaps onto his face, and find myself laughing as I make an ungraceful lunge for the last one.

Another hand seizes it at the same time, and I look up into Fletcher's deep brown eyes.

He lets go at once, standing hastily. He holds a few of the drawings, a bit crumpled now.

'Here,' he says, looking somewhere over my shoulder.

'Thanks.'

'Are these yours, Miss Kestle?' Gryff asks, squinting down at the page before handing it back.

'Just some doodles, for Davy,' I say quickly, folding them into my bag. 'I'm years out of practice.'

'Doesn't look so to me. Wouldn't you say, Jem?' There's a sort of sly, gleeful look on Gryff's face that's impossible to ignore, even though Fletcher only nods. 'You'll have to do us a drawing of the Helm. As a keepsake.'

I smile back. 'Any time.'

'Well now,' he clears his throat. 'Lucas is down by the jetty. Like as not he'll give you a ride over.'

There's an awkward moment as he stares expectantly at his grandson. Finally, Jem extends a hand and I take it, feeling the calluses on his fingers, across the palm.

'Safe travels,' he mutters, before striding into the pub, head bowed as if the storm is still raging around him.

Gryff's right, I tell myself, watching them go back into the warm. *It's not my problem.*

Unlike the Fletchers, Lucas greets me happily. I watch him load the last few crates of fish onto the boat, the pungent smell of brine rising around me. 'Not like Sunday, eh?' he says with a grin as we set off across the calm stretch of water between islands.

It's a perfect December day, the air crisp as chilled champagne, the low winter sun sparkling on the waves, the sky and the sea both so blue it's almost unreal. White gulls and curlews and guillemots cry and wheel and I breathe deep, filling my lungs with salt and light, as if I'll be able to carry it all away with me.

It's still early when we reach St Mary's. I risk turning on my phone – back to 11 per cent battery thanks to Lucas's jury-rigged charger on the boat – to find it crammed with notifications and messages. A lot of them are work emails, more than one of them from my boss asking how long this emergency will take, reminding me that I have to show her the completed presentation for Hunter-Thorpe, with accompanying reports, before I can even *think* of being allowed to go to the meeting. Annoyed, I switch it off and shove it into my pocket. Plenty of time to work on the train. *Not yet*, I think, staring out over the achingly blue bay. *Not quite yet.*

The shops of Hugh Town are bustling today, the windows merry with decorations. The main street is blocked off with some old cones and an ancient pick-up truck and soon I see why: people in high-vis jackets are busy hanging Christmas lights across the narrow street.

''iss 'estle!' someone shouts down from a rickety cherry picker. It takes me a moment to realise they're calling my name.

Peering up, I see Lou, the pilot, holding a hammer in one hand, a nail in the other, a string of fairy lights in her mouth.

''eticia's 'ooking 'or 'oo!' she calls down.

'What?' I laugh.

'I 'ed . . .' She gives up, letting the string fall from her mouth. 'I said, Leticia's looking for you.'

'I wanted to say goodbye, too. Is she at the office?'

'Yeah!'

I frown. 'Wait, aren't you flying me back in a while?'

She waggles the hammer. 'Woman of many talents, me. Olly!' she bellows down at a bespectacled young man, who stands arm-deep in a tangle of lights. 'The yellow ones! Not the green, they're for the church. The *yellow* ones!'

Smiling, I make my way to the office and try the door, but it's locked.

'Leticia?' I call. 'Are you there?'

No answer. With a sigh, I step back onto the street only to be hit by the scent of freshly baked bread, oven-caught currants, hot sugar. I follow it, nose twitching, and find a bakery, its window piled high with gleaming saffron buns and crusty new loaves, sugar-dusted stollen and stack after stack of crisp mince pies. Shouldering my bag, I step inside.

A few minutes later I puff up the hill towards the grand grey Penhallow House, a paper bag of still-warm saffron buns in my hands. It's early, but hopefully Olivia and Sam won't mind. I let myself in through the gate, and cross the gardens, frost lingering in the shadows. At the top of the stone steps Philip the bulldog sits blinking in the sunlight, wearing his little tartan coat. He struggles to his feet when he sees me, his tail wagging.

'Hello, old man,' I greet, stroking his ears.

Blinking his round, rheumy eyes at me, he waddles through the front door, which stands ajar.

'Hello?' I call on the threshold. 'Olivia? Sam?'

The only answer comes from Philip, who gives a wheezy snort and trundles off into the study. I follow him in.

'Hello?' I call again, poking my head around the door, but the room is empty, save for Philip, who flumps down onto a large dog cushion.

'Where is everyone, eh?' I ask.

I'm about to turn away, to call up the stairs, when something on the big oak desk catches my attention: a meticulously drawn map of the islands. Fascinated, I lean down to take in the details, the names of the rocks and reefs, the currents between them, the points and hills and ruins and secret coves. Resting on top of that map is another, smaller one. My heart gives a strange squeeze when I realise it's of Morgelyn.

Smiling sadly I trace it with a fingertip, the harbour, the jetty, the Helm, the headland overlooking Davy's bay. A square marks out Davy's cottage, a dotted line encircling the cove labelled D. PENHALLOW.

I pick up the map to look more closely only to find a piece of acetate attached to the paper, some kind of overlay. Curious, I let it fall over the page.

PENHALLOW LUXURY HOTEL AND SPA, a box at the top reads and, for a moment, I'm not sure what I'm seeing. On this drawing, the entire island has been transformed. The pub is gone, replaced by a long building, labelled HOTEL AND SPA. The harbour and jetty have been remodelled into a grand pier, wharves jutting out like fingers into the sea.

POTENTIAL FOR 200 MOORINGS, the caption reads.

I grip the map, following the depiction of a new, two-lane carriageway that carves straight across the headland where the gorse now flowers, ending in *Penhallow's Yacht Clubhouse and Private Beach.*

Davy's cottage is gone. Instead, a sketch of a modern, two-storey building takes up the entire cove, which has been widened into an artificial curve. *Imported sand*, the plan notes.

Stomach thudding with nausea, I drop the map and start to search the desk, mind skittering over the words, the drawings. I grab up a letter from an architectural firm, and can hardly make sense of what I'm reading: *approved plans for redevelopment – ownership of property – commence immediately in the New Year to be completed for season—*

'Mina!'

The letter slips from my fingers as I look up in shock. Sam stands in the doorway, her hair wrapped in a towel.

'I didn't hear you come in,' she says. 'Livvy's at a meeting, but she shouldn't be long.'

I don't answer, staring at her, my mind racing. Abruptly, I remember Olivia sitting in the cottage yesterday, her reluctance when I told her about my plan to keep Davy in his own home, the way she said, *We don't know what will happen.* About her offer to take control of the guardianship, how keen she was that I transfer it to her. How Elodie looked at me in disgust when I said I'd left Murr in her care. Watching me, Sam's smile falters.

'Mina, are you all right?'

'What is this?' I demand, thrusting the letter towards her.

Looking at the desk, her face pales. 'It's . . . those are private.'

'From who? Me? Davy? If this goes ahead it'll destroy his cottage. It will destroy the whole island.'

'No, it's not like that!' She steps towards me, her face twisted. 'It'll be good for the island, it'll bring in jobs, more money—'

'What about people's homes? What about the land?'

Her grey eyes are wide. 'We've considered that, Mina. The estate is going to make a donation to a wildlife fund, to offset the building work. We have a responsibility to use the land to its fullest advantage.'

I can hear Olivia's words in her mouth so clearly that I let out a harsh laugh, throwing the letter back onto the desk. 'Well, you can tell your sister to forget about it. Davy would never agree to this. Never.'

'But Mina, you don't understand.' Sam's voice stops me as I shove past her into the hall. 'He already has.'

*

The blood pounds in my ears as I race down the hill, back towards town. How could I have been so stupid? Why didn't I question any of it? I almost knock an old woman flying as I hurl myself around the corner and up the steps of Strout & Daughter, Solicitors.

'Leticia!' I yell, hammering on the door. 'Leticia, are you there?'

I swear in relief when I see movement, and Leticia pulls open the door. Today she's wearing a festive jumper with a large snowman on it.

'Mina?' she asks, frowning at the state of me.

'In Olivia's study,' I gasp, stumbling into the office. 'Plans for Morgelyn, for Davy's cottage. They're going to destroy it. And Sam said, she told me Davy knows. That he signed off on it . . .'

I collapse into a seat, catching my breath, waiting for Leticia to scoff, to tell me that the Penhallows are trying their luck, that's all. Instead, she sinks down behind the desk with a deep sigh. Dread washes through me.

'It's not true?'

She nods miserably. 'I just came from a meeting with Olivia Penhallow. She showed me the power of attorney application. She said that Davy signed it weeks ago, before he collapsed.'

I stare, my heart thudding. 'But . . . even if that's true, the plans. Davy would never give permission. She's lying about him agreeing to it. She *has* to be lying.'

'I saw the signature myself. It's Davy's.'

'What about my guardianship?' I grip the desk. 'Surely that counts for something?'

'It'll be superseded by the power of attorney.' She rubs at her face, smudging her glittery eye shadow. 'I'm sorry, Mina. I don't understand it, either. Davy never mentioned it to me.'

I can't help it, the tears that have been gathering in my eyes start to fall, hot tears of frustration and anger and sadness for

Davy. Leticia hurries from the desk and folds me into a hug, and for a moment I just hold onto her, my head buried in her jumper that smells of washing powder and fried bacon and rose perfume, telling her about Davy's letters to me, about how my father hid every single one. After a few minutes, she fishes a tissue from her sleeve and I blow my nose, cleaning up my face as best I can.

'All these years,' I tell her, thickly. 'I thought *he* had forgotten about *me*.'

She sits back into her own chair with a heavy sigh. 'This should never have happened. I wish now I'd checked up on Davy sooner. I almost went over there last week, but my youngest was home ill from school.'

Last week, I think, blotting my eyes. Last week I had no idea about any of this. My biggest worry had been whether I'd find myself unemployed by the time the new year rolled around ...

Abruptly, something clicks in my mind.

Last week.

I grab my handbag from the floor. It's in an even worse state now, full of bits and pieces from the cottage: shells, stones, the jar of honey, a toothbrush, Davy's letters, the drawings. But there, right at the bottom, my fingers find paper, and I drag out the crumpled envelope, the one I opened what feels like a hundred years ago in the bathrooms at the office Christmas party.

'Julia,' I tell Leticia, thrusting it at her, pointing to the flowered sticker.

'*Julia*?' she blinks, lost.

'My stepmother. *She* was the one who forwarded this on. My dad was away at a conference. Or he would have sent it back like all the others.' I peer at the postmark. 'What day did Davy collapse?'

'Last Monday.'

I hold it up to show her. 'This was sent on the same day.'

She peers. 'He must have collapsed on his way back from the post office.'

'But doesn't this change things?' I scramble inside the envelope, pricking myself on the piece of dried sea holly once again. 'Look, in his note, Davy asks me to look after Murr. Isn't that proof that he wants me to look after the cottage, too? As late as last week?'

The look of defeat on Leticia's face is unmistakable. 'It's not enough. Penhallow has filed an official document with the Office of the Public Guardian. No one will take an unsigned note over that. And once power of attorney is granted . . .'

'They can do anything they want.'

She nods glumly.

I stare down at the envelope, thinking of Davy struggling to the island's post office with the key and the note, putting all of his strength and hope into just five words.

Mina, please look after her.

Leticia starts as I jump to my feet, pushing the chair back.

'This isn't going to happen. I won't let it. We have to fight them on this.'

'We can't.'

'Why not?'

Her pink-cheeked face is twisted. 'The Penhallows own half these islands. They own this building. They own my house, my sister's house, my nephew's. Olivia Penhallow could easily evict us in retaliation, and we'd have nowhere to go. We couldn't afford to stay here, Mina.'

Furious, I grab my bag.

'Where are you going?' Leticia says as I jerk open the door.

'To the hospital.'

'What about your flight?' she calls as I run down the steps.

CHAPTER TWELVE

I dash through the streets, emerging onto the road that winds along the coast. The winter sun blazes, turning the sea blue-silver with brilliance, but I don't have any mind for it, nor for the white painted houses, the palm trees wound around with Christmas lights. Instead, I stride up the cliff path, taking out my phone and dialling a number with the once-again dwindling battery.

Olivia Penhallow's phone rings and rings, before going to voicemail.

'Coward!' I yell, scaring a nearby gull.

I want to hurl the phone over the cliff and down into the glittering sea below, but I don't. Instead, I stuff it into my bag and march on through the hospital's doors, sweaty and furious.

'Davy Penhallow,' I announce, breathing hard.

I recognise the ward sister from my previous visit. She's wearing a Santa hat, though her expression is anything but jolly. 'I'm sorry, Miss Kestle,' she frowns. 'No visits today.'

The words startle me out of my rage. 'What? Is he OK? Has something happened?'

'He's fine. In fact, he woke up briefly this morning. That's a very good sign.'

'He did?' A wave of relief rushes over me. There won't have to be a fight, not if Davy's awake. 'Did he say anything? How is he now?'

'He did try to talk, but it seems his speech has been affected by the stroke. That's not unusual,' she rushes to assure me. 'And, like I said, he was conscious, which is an excellent sign.'

'Thank God.' I force myself to take a breath. 'So when can I visit? Later, or . . .?'

She clears her throat, looking down at her notes. 'I'm afraid it's not possible.'

I stare at her. 'What do you mean?'

This is obviously a conversation she was hoping not to have. 'Ms Penhallow has said that Mr Penhallow is not to be disturbed.'

Anger shimmers across my skin. 'I won't disturb him. I just want to see him.'

'I'm sorry, I can't let you in.'

'This is ridiculous. I'm next of kin, I'm his goddaughter.'

The smile she gives me is pained. 'I'm afraid we have to respect the wishes of Mr Penhallow's *immediate* family.'

'And what about Davy?' I demand. 'What if he wants to see me? Surely it's up to him.'

'Of course, if he indicated as much. But he hasn't.' She gives me a sympathetic look. 'I suggest you speak to Olivia. I'm sure all of this can be sorted out.'

Olivia.

I turn away. Of course she's trying to stop me from seeing Davy. She's wanted me out of the cottage and off the islands from the second we met – why else would she have come looking for me that day? Why else did she want to keep me close? It wasn't kindness. It was strategy.

I pull the handful of drawings from my bag. 'Can I leave these for him at least?'

The ward sister's expression softens, a little. 'Of course. I'll put them in his room.'

Down on the quayside, I call Paola with the last of my battery.

'Mina!' She answers immediately in a rush of relief. 'I've tried to call you, like, a thousand times.'

'Sorry, sorry.'

On the roof of the phone box behind me, a seagull starts shrieking, giving another bird a piece of its mind.

'Mina,' Paola's voice is hushed as she leans into the phone. I can hear the office hubbub in the background. 'Please tell me you are on that plane.'

I grimace. 'I am not on that plane.'

'*Cavolo!*' she swears. 'Is it the airline? Let me look, I'll see if I can find another service that might be able to—'

'No. It's not the airline, Paola. It's me.' I touch the cold pane of the phone box and take a deep breath. 'I'm calling to say that I won't be there tomorrow, to meet Hunter-Thorpe.'

'What the hell?' The frustration in her voice gives way to worry. 'Is everything OK? Has something happened?'

So much. 'I just can't leave now.'

There's a silence, followed by a clattering of doors. Paola walking out of the office. I hear a rush of air, traffic, as if she's stepped outside. 'Mina,' she says, louder. 'That meeting is probably the only thing keeping Marianne from firing you in the new year.'

I close my eyes. 'I know.'

'And? Don't you care?'

For some reason, a laugh bubbles in my chest. 'No, I don't think I do.'

She swears again and I hear the sound of her lighter flicking, a deep inhale. 'Look,' she says. 'I can't cover for you any more. The bosses are already pissed off you're not here. And when Marianne hears you've ditched the meeting—'

All at once, everything seems clearer than it has in years. 'Thank you, P,' I say abruptly.

'For what?'

'For caring. I mean it, thank you.'

She snorts. 'You always were a weirdo.' I hear her inhale again. 'All right. I'll tell Marianne. But you owe me for this!'

'I know. Name your price.'

'Cocktails at Vincent's. Three rounds on you, *at least*.'

'Deal,' I laugh, pressing the phone to my cheek, wishing I could see her rolling her eyes.

She chuckles, before her tone changes, turning softer. 'You are OK, though, aren't you, Mina?'

'Yes,' I murmur into the phone, looking out towards Morgelyn. 'I think I'm going to be fine.'

When she's gone, I spend a long minute staring at the phone's flashing battery, before switching it off. Then, taking another breath, I step inside the phone box and slot in a fifty pence piece, dialling a number that's printed on an old, faded poster taped to the inside of the phone box.

'Gryff?' I say, when a voice answers. 'It's Mina. Would you mind meeting me? I need to talk to you about Morgelyn. It's important.'

Later – after blagging a ride across the water from a young man in a skiff who turns out to be one of Lucas's friends – I step inside the Helm Inn to find it crammed with people. Some I recognise – the lady from the village shop, the old man with the distant blue eyes, the two older women who laughed at me that first day, but there are new faces, too – some in rubber boots and old, knitted jumpers, others in smart shirts or overalls, as if they've dropped everything to come here straight from work. For a second I hesitate on the doorstep, heat flooding my chilled face, before Gryff spots me and bustles over, wearing a rainbow-knitted waistcoat over a Hawaiian shirt.

'Gryff,' I hiss, 'I said I needed to talk to *you*.'

His weather-beaten face creases in an apologetic smile. 'I know. Only, you said it was about the island, so I mentioned it to Reni from the shop, and she told Veronika, who told Barry . . .'

'Who told me,' an older man says, seizing my hand. He wears a battered flat cap, his fingernails stained green. 'Stan Purdue from the flower farm. And my husband, Luis.'

A second man with a salt and pepper beard opens his mouth to ask a question, but before he can a large woman with a wind-reddened face and fingers thick enough to break rocks seizes my hand. 'Linda Blythe,' she booms. 'Believe you've met my lad, Lucas. And those are my other two, Lila and Lydia,' she says pointing out two younger women in the window seat, one with a toddler on her lap.

I nod and smile, my head spinning from all the faces, and try to retreat towards the bar, only to collide with someone near the fireplace, spilling tea all over the floor.

'Sorry,' I gasp to the man standing there.

'No harm done,' he answers, brushing his jumper down. He's tall and lean, with a smooth shaved head and huge round glasses. 'Mo Said,' he smiles, extending a hand. 'I'm the archivist at the local museum.'

'Nice to meet you,' I stutter, overwhelmed. 'Nice to meet you all.'

'Coming through!' a voice calls, and people cram to one side as Elodie emerges, trays in both hands.

'Ahh!' Linda Blythe claps her hands together. 'Snacks.'

'Is this an emergency meeting or a party?' another woman grumbles, even as she reaches towards the plate of mince pies.

'Care to try, Miss Kestle?'

I look around to see Gryff offering me a bowl of Gryff's Cuisine fish paste. Across the room, Reni from the shop shakes her head in warning.

'Ah, I—'

Elodie grabs my elbow and tows me towards the bar. 'Don't eat it, you'll be tasting shrimp for weeks,' she murmurs, before plonking a large glass of red wine in front of me. 'Are you ready?'

'For what?' I almost shriek.

'You're here to talk about the island, right?' She raises dark brows. 'So talk.'

Taking a swig of wine, I nod.

Decisively, she reaches up to clang the old ship's bell that hangs behind the bar. 'All right, all right,' she calls. 'Settle down, we've got important things to discuss.'

The hubbub immediately quietens, people shoving for seats, craning to see. 'Right,' Elodie says loudly. 'You probably have an idea of why we're here. Most of you already know about our problems with the Penhallow Estate.' There's a chorus of mutters and groans, and she holds up her hands. 'But now it seems like the problem is bigger than we thought.' She gives me a nod. Heat rushes into my face as every pair of eyes in the pub turns my way.

'Go on,' Elodie encourages.

With a deep breath, I stand and tell the room about everything I saw in the Penhallows' study – the estate plans, the island-wide hotel, the destruction of the cove and Davy's cottage to make way for a yacht club. The fact that Davy supposedly signed off on it.

The second I finish speaking the pub explodes into noise.

'I can't believe it, not of Davy.'

'. . . money-grubbing, land-grabbing, speedboat-driving . . .'

'Knew there was something up. Didn't Janice say she'd seen an application ...'

'... gilet-wearing, champagne-quaffing ...'

'Would a hotel be *such* a bad thing?'

'It would in the Penhallows' hands. And didn't you hear Mina? It would destroy the Helm, the cove, the headland.'

'It would be the end of Morgelyn,' Gryff says, turning one of his jars of pâté around. 'It would be the end of Murr.'

At that, everyone stops talking.

'Leticia said Davy wanted to name me guardian of the cottage, and of Murr,' I say quietly. 'I don't know what will happen to Davy, or to Morgelyn, but I'm going to do my best to honour his wishes.'

Chatter breaks out across the room again, but this time, people come forward to squeeze my arm, to shake my hand, to tell me they're with me.

'We could phone the government office Leticia mentioned,' Stan Purdue says. 'Report a problem with the power of attorney application?'

'I'll see what's happening at the council,' Lydia Blythe offers.

'My mate Liam works at the hospital, sure he can help us get in to see Davy,' Lucas says, phone already in hand.

'What about the land itself?' Mo Said pushes his glasses up his nose. 'From everything I've read, there are signs of a very old settlement here. Perhaps there's a way we can get it listed, protect the whole island? I know several groups who have tried in the past ...'

I look around at them, all of these people I barely know, talking, arguing, looking things up on their phones. They're all here, even with their own problems, ready to fight for their home, for an old man and his cat and his cottage.

'Thank you,' I tell them, chest aching. 'I really appreciate it. I just wish I'd seen through Olivia sooner. I feel like such an idiot.'

'You weren't to know,' Gryff says kindly.

I take a gulp of wine. 'She came to the cottage yesterday, all smiles and lilies and posh biscuits. I thought she was being *nice* but she was probably scouting the place—'

'What?' Elodie lets a tap fall back, halfway through pouring a pint.

'I said I thought she was being nice.'

'No. About the lilies.'

I make a face. 'Trying to butter me up, I guess.'

'And you left them in the cottage?'

I stare at her. 'Yes, why?'

'It's just ... aren't lilies toxic to cats?'

My stomach plummets when I think of the vase, crammed so full with lilies that their scent filled the whole place.

'She wouldn't. Not deliberately.' But at the same time I remember Leticia's voice, that first day in her office, telling me, *In the event of the cat's demise, ownership of the estate would pass to the guardian ...*

I slam the glass down and dash out of the door, only this time I'm not alone. Elodie is the fastest, barging out of the pub's back door and sprinting up the sandy path in her Doc Martens. Mo Said follows, already searching for information on his phone as we run. Gryff puffs behind us, yelling for us not to wait for him.

We rush through the furze paths, over the headland, my throat aching in the cold air.

'Murr?' I yell, as we skid down the path and onto the beach.

Leaving the others to call and search the hollows in the heather, I grab the key from behind the bowl and jam it into the lock with shaking hands.

Please be OK, please, please ...

'Murr?' I gasp, staggering inside. But the cottage is empty, only the lilies, a dozen of them, striped and livid in the vase, their pollen dusting the tabletop. The others tumble after me, peering into the bedroom, looking under chairs, but I can *feel* she isn't here, as if the cottage has lost its heart and is just four walls made of stone, not the brimming, living place I know it to be.

'She isn't here,' I tell them. 'Where is she?'

Gryff pants down to the cottage, his face red, sweat streaming from his temples. Elodie goes to him at once, pulling out a chair for him to collapse into.

'Well?' he wheezes.

Sick, I shake my head. Just then, I hear a squeak, a thud of wood. Heart racing in my chest, I turn around.

Murr comes strolling into the kitchen, only to stop when she sees all the people there, letting out a questioning meow. With a noise that's half laugh and half sob, I scoop her into my arms and hold her big, heavy, fluffy body tightly as Elodie seizes the lilies and stomps down to the shore, turfing them onto the waves, while Mo smiles in relief, saying Murr is obviously far too clever to be caught out by a trick like that, and Gryff is reaching into his pocket to produce a jar of potted shrimp.

Only then does it strike me that someone is missing from the company. Someone who tried to warn me about Penhallow, who came to feed Murr from the very start, whose picture hangs on Davy's wall. Who I might have been wrong about all along.

'Elodie,' I say, as Murr purrs and rubs her face against my chin. 'Where can I find your brother?'

CHAPTER THIRTEEN

In the rain, the bay at the other end of the island is deserted. It's tiny, smaller even than Davy's beach, a crescent moon of wet sand among worn rocks, blue-grey sea holly growing in other-worldly clusters. Today the sea looks like ruffled silk, glowing with its own light.

A wooden building like a fishing shack nestles among the dunes, a ribbon of smoke coiling from its chimney. I take a steadying breath.

'He's got a streak of pride, that's for sure.' Elodie's voice comes back to me, sitting around the table in Davy's kitchen. *'But most of all, I think he's scared.'*

I cross the damp sand in the wellingtons I borrowed from Elodie – only one size too big – leaving deep prints that the waddling gulls eye with interest. The garden around the cabin is littered with flotsam; huge twisted logs, bits of net, metal, mounds of glimmering sea glass. Beneath a tin-roofed porch a bench waits, as if someone likes to sit here to watch the tide. The planks creak as I step up to knock.

'I haven't finished the smaller one yet, Mo,' comes a yell, 'but if you come back in—'

The door swings open and Jem Fletcher stops on the threshold, staring. He wears a tattered blue fisherman's jumper, clung all over with sawdust.

'I brought these,' I blurt.

In a paper bag are two of Elodie's famous festive pasties. I know she's spoken to him about everything that's happened, but that doesn't mean he's changed his mind about me. For a long moment he stares. Then, finally, the corner of his mouth twitches. He clearly knows a peace offering when he sees one.

'Cup of coffee?' he asks awkwardly.

'Thanks.'

He steps back. 'Come in. Sorry about the mess everywhere.'

I kick off my boots on the mat, staring around. It looks more like an artist's studio than a house. Pieces of driftwood and timber stand about the place, sawdust gathers in the corners in small drifts. The place smells of fresh wood-shavings and smoke, the warm musk of tar and varnish, the distant mineral tang of seaweed. And all around are sketches – pinned to the walls, weighed down by rocks. The windowsill is cluttered with little items. Enthralled, I reach to pick one up. It's shaped like a gull.

'Scrimshaws,' Jem says, as he places a coffee pot on a stove in the corner. 'Sailors used to make them out of whale bone, but I just use driftwood, plastic, anything that washes up, really.'

Smoothing the gull's wing, I suddenly realise why the carving is so familiar. 'I found one of these on Davy's mantelpiece. A cat. Did you make it?'

He rubs his neck, as if embarrassed. 'For Christmas, once.'

As he chucks a few offcuts into the stove, I wander through the rest of the room, examining the driftwood pieces. Some are faintly recognisable as figures or animals, others so abstract that I find myself lost in tracing their patterns; like the ripple of sunlight through water, like the slow swaying of seaweed. I'm especially drawn to one – a piece of sea-worn wood that looks like a woman turning, a crest over her head that could be a wave, or a leaping creature.

'Morgelyn and her cat,' Jem says beside me, brushing some sawdust from the sculpture.

'Like Davy's story.'

'Not just Davy's. It's an old tale around here.'

'Explains why Murr is such a local celebrity.'

He only smiles. 'Milk?'

'Yes, thanks.'

We take our coffee out to the porch. I wrap my hands around the mug, watching as the winter light rakes across the sea.

'I knew Penhallow was up to something,' Jem says after a long silence. 'Ever since she started trying to push Gramps and Elodie out of the pub. And now this with Davy.' He turns the mug in his hands. 'I think you're right about that signature. There's no way it can be real. Davy would have told me.'

I meet his eyes. 'If Davy's awake he can just deny everything. Which is why we have to try and see him.'

He raises an eyebrow at me. 'We? Don't you have to get back to London?'

'No. I decided that this is more important.'

'Is your work OK with that?'

I smile into my coffee. 'Probably not.'

'You don't seem too bothered.'

'I'm not. Technically I'm doing everything wrong, but for the first time in years, it *feels* right.'

For a while we sit in silence, watching the gulls wheel, the hush of the waves.

'Davy never gave up on you, you know.' Jem's voice is soft. 'He talked about you sometimes, usually when he'd had a few too many. Told me stories about those months you and your mum lived with him, about how he felt like he had a family again. I've lost track of the number of times I offered to help him look for you. I even tried a few times on my own, searching for Mina Martinovszky, but never had any luck. Now I know why.' He looks over. 'Davy always said that you'd come back, if you felt called to.'

We're sitting elbow to elbow, and this close I can see how deep brown his eyes are, how there's a fleck of sawdust in his black curls. I catch his scent; smoke and soap and sun-warmed wood and clean cotton on skin.

'Thank you,' I tell him, my heart aching. 'For looking after him.'

He only nods, before seeming to come to some kind of conclusion. 'What are you doing now?'

'I'm meant to be meeting Mo at the museum. And then we're going to try and see Davy again. Why?'

'Can I show you something, later? I think it might be important.'

'To Davy?'

He shakes his head with a smile. 'No. To you.'

Mo is waiting for me at the museum, a strangely modern building in the centre of Hugh Town. A vast, colourful knitted cardigan swamps his smart waistcoat and shirt. 'A gift from Gryff,' he explains, a little sheepishly. 'This place is like an icebox in the winter. We mostly keep the heating off, apart from the atmospherically controlled cases, to save money.'

Our footsteps echo strangely, a lonely sound in this place where so many memories clamour. The museum is crammed floor to rafters with objects. Paintings and life buoys hang from the banisters, lobster pots are stacked in corners, every inch of wall and floor space taken up by another display of photographs or archaeological finds. Mo leads the way up a staircase, then around a crowded balcony, and finally through a door marked ARCHIVES.

'Here we are,' he says, as strip lights ping into life overhead.

The room is small, stuffed with bookshelves and archive boxes. The window blinds are firmly down, and the place smells of dust and cardboard and the sugary must of old paper. A wooden table stands against one wall, an ancient microfilm reader at the end.

'Is this . . .?' I ask.

'Records from across the islands,' Mo says, his face alight. 'Curate's ledgers, letters, estate documents, you name it.'

'I don't know where to start.'

'Then it's a good job I do.' He grins.

I watch as he hustles about, extracting a few long cardboard tubes from the shelves, hefting out ledgers, pulling on a pair of white cotton gloves. He's obviously in his element.

'How do you know where anything is?'

'Oh, there's a system,' he says. 'Though it's taken me a good few months to get to grips with what's here.' He pushes his glasses up his nose. 'My friends on the mainland thought I was mad for taking this job – it pays a pittance – but I couldn't resist. It's my first curatorship. And there's so much here, so many stories. But for today –' he clears a space on the table '– I thought we'd start with the maps. They're usually a good indicator of historical landmarks over time. This one's from the eighteen hundreds.'

He unrolls a large, yellowed piece of paper. It's a hand-drawn map of the Isles of Scilly, every rock and cove.

'There's ancient history all over these islands,' Mo says, hovering a finger over the surface. 'Some say they were the lost "Tin Isles", where people came to trade from all over the world – Greece, Phoenicia . . .'

I lean in to see the map better as Mo points out ancient

monuments and standing stones, grave sites and hut circles, dolmens, menhirs, cairns.

'And here's Morgelyn,' he says.

I can see Davy's cove. But there's no writing to indicate ownership, like on Penhallow's map, just a strange circular symbol.

'What does that mean?' I ask.

'I can only guess that whoever drew this map wanted to note that there was something important about the site. Unfortunately, they don't go into detail. However –' Mo's eyes spark '– I had some luck when I went further back.'

Very gingerly, he takes down another folder. 'This is one of the oldest maps in the collection. Donated by a vicar in the last century.' He peels back layers of protective tissue paper. The map below looks ancient, the paper crumbling in the corners. The islands are drawn as basic shapes, the ports labelled in cramped, indecipherable writing. I make out St Mary's and St Martin's before Mo touches my arm and points. 'Look.'

I peer closely at the representation of Morgelyn. Davy's cove is featured, but this time there's also a spiral of writing; not in the same heavy ink as the rest of the map but thinner, scratchier, as if added later or in haste.

'Lanbenglas,' I whisper, reading the first word. It lingers on my lips like salt spray, familiar, as if I've said it a thousand times before. Then I remember the man on the beach, with his faraway blue eyes. 'I know that name. There was an old man on Morgelyn, he pointed at the headland, said something about the gorse growing?'

Mo raises his eyebrows. 'That sounds like Mr Tredugget. People say he knows everything about the islands. I suppose I shouldn't be surprised that he remembers the old names.'

I look back to that hurried writing. 'What does it *mean*?'

'Lanbenglas could be a name, which is useful.'

'How come?'

'Names can tell us quite a lot. Like Morgelyn. Did you know it means "sea holly"?' I shake my head, remembering Davy's yuletide decorations, the sprig that always hangs above his door. 'Or Tresco,' Mo goes on. 'That comes from "Enys Scaw", "island of elder trees." Which means we could be onto something here. I think "Lan" usually means "holy" or "sacred", like a site of worship.'

Hope rises in me. 'And that would make it a site of historical interest?'

'Maybe.' He straightens up. 'Wait here, I'm going to find Stevie, one of the volunteers. If this was Latin or Greek or Arabic or Aramaic we'd be fine, but my Cornish is still a work in progress.'

Before I can ask he's out of the door, footsteps echoing away. My ears ring in the sudden silence. Lanbenglas. There's something about the word that feels so familiar. I hover my fingers above it, trying to imagine whose hand dipped a quill in ink and wrote the letters here. Perhaps a boy – perhaps an apprentice . . .

His master's work was laid over the table in the ship's cabin, fine new paper weighed down with stones from the beach, the smell of fresh gall ink in the air. Roll it carefully, seal it with wax and ribbon and take it to the Lord of the Islands. That was his task.

And yet one unlabelled cove gnawed at him, for he knew what – who – it belonged to. Not the Lord of the Islands. Not the King. It belonged to her.

Closing his eyes, he pictured the cove, with its cott made of grey stone. He smelled the gorse and the ling and the strange flowers that scatter the shore in summer, grown from the tossed ballast of departing ships. He heard the whispers of the islanders about the woman who lived there with her familiar – his mother, the pellar woman, the white witch. He heard again her voice singing on a Midwinter's Night, mingling with the sound of the waves, a cat's gentle purr. He felt it in his chest, the low rumbles of the cat who slept beside him, his best friend, keeping him safe.

The boy remembered his island, home until he left at eleven years old, to take to the ships and make his fortune, before he was lucky enough to be apprenticed to the cartographer in Penzance. He remembered and his heart ached.

And so he did the only thing he could: he took up his master's fine quill pen, and while the ship rocked and groaned around him, he added hasty words to the cove, not in Latin or English but in another tongue, one that the Lord of the Islands did not speak. He did what he could to honour, to remember.

Then, hearing his master's step on the deck, the boy scattered sand and rolled the map, sealing in his secret.

'Mina?'

I jerk away from the table so fast that my head spins. When my eyes clear, I see Mo standing by the door, someone behind him.

'Mina, this is Stevie. Their Cornish is much better than mine.'

Blinking, I hold out my hand. Stevie can't be more than twenty, with cropped hair dyed bright red and thick-framed glasses.

'Thanks for helping,' I say. 'Hope we're not disturbing you?'

'Makes a change from avoiding my dissertation,' they grin. 'Now, where's this writing?'

We squash together over the table, Mo fetching a magnifying glass to help.

'Yep, that's definitely Cornish,' Stevie confirms.

'We think Lanbenglas is a name,' I say. 'I'm sure one of the old men on the island mentioned it.'

'Old names tend to stick around. And Mo's right, "Lan" means sacred place. As for the rest . . .' Stevie squints. '"Ben" is tricky; it could mean "woman" or "walks", I'm not sure. And "glas" is the same. It either means "grey" or "the colour of the sea".'

'So altogether?'

They think. 'It could tell us that this place was sacred to one who walks there, who is grey or sea-coloured, and probably female.'

I stare at the map, hearing Davy's voice. 'It's like the story again. Morgelyn and her cat. Davy told it to me, years ago.'

Mo smiles. 'An old tale, that one. I've heard it, too. Maybe it's what remains of a pre-Christian belief system, a local deity, a sea goddess, perhaps?'

'And the writing?' I ask Stevie eagerly. 'What does that say?'

'*Yma hi orth diwedhva an vledhen goth ha dallethva an vledhen nowydh,*' they read. 'Um, "She is at the old year's ending and the new year's beginning." Something like that.'

A shiver runs through me from scalp to heel. I've heard those words before, I know it. But where?

'Will this help us?' I ask Mo.

'It might be enough to register the site as one of potential historical significance.'

'And that would stop the development?'

He shakes his head. 'Slow it, maybe. We'd need some sort of physical proof to legally protect it.'

I stare down at the map, pushing away a wave of frustration. It's something, at least. One step closer.

CHAPTER FOURTEEN

I walk across the hospital car park with feigned casualness, approaching from the back rather than the main entrance.

When I reach a fire door, I text *Here* to the number Lucas gave me.

My heart thuds as I wait. Is this illegal? A few minutes later, just as I'm about to lose my nerve, the door creaks open and a young man in a nurse's uniform steps outside, lighting a cigarette. Glancing sidelong at me, he gives a tiny nod, before strolling away.

Darting forwards, I catch the closing fire door and slip inside. The corridor beyond is quiet, with a green lino floor and metal cages full of laundry. Nerves thrumming, I hurry along it, expecting someone to appear at any moment.

At a set of double doors I stop, peering beyond. The hospital isn't big, but already I'm lost. Which way was Davy's room?

'Hey,' a sharp voice says, and I turn, guilty as a criminal, to see a man in a porter's uniform leaning out of a doorway. 'This is staff only.'

'Sorry,' I say, pushing the doors open.

'Wait!' the porter calls.

I race down the hallway beyond and up a set of stairs, past more doors and finally find myself on a corridor that looks familiar. Wasn't Davy in a private room, halfway down?

There, a closed door with a marker-pen name tag: D. PENHALLOW. Smiling triumphantly, I step inside.

'Davy!'

The room is empty. The bed has been stripped of sheets, the machines silent. Even the locker stands open, cleared out.

'No,' I whisper in horror. 'Please, no.'

'Excuse me!' The ward sister appears in the doorway, the porter behind her. 'What do you think you're doing?'

'Where is he?' I demand, eyes stinging. 'My godfather, is he . . .?'

At once, the ward sister's expression shifts from annoyance to sympathy. 'I thought you'd been told. Mr Penhallow was transferred this morning.'

'Transferred? To where? A different room?'

'No, to a private facility.' She obviously mistakes my shock for incomprehension because she goes on. 'The doctors agreed that Mr Penhallow was stable enough to be moved, so he was released into the care of his relatives.'

'*What?*'

She clears her throat, obviously uncomfortable. 'Like I said, he has been transferred to a private hospital. I'm sure he's receiving excellent care.'

'Where have they taken him?'

'I'm afraid I can't—'

'Where?'

She glances at the door and sighs. 'To a hospital on the mainland. That's all I can say.'

*

'What the hell is Olivia playing at?' I rage, thumping the cluttered desk, sending a mini Christmas tree tumbling. 'Surely she can't *do* that?'

Leticia rights the tree. 'Unfortunately, she can. She's Davy's closest next of kin on the islands. That means she's able to make decisions about his care while Davy is incapable of doing so himself.'

'But the nurse said he was conscious, that he had been improving.' I look around at the others, all crowded into Leticia's little office; Elodie, pale with anger, Lou, glumly eating her way through a packet of Hobnobs in the corner, having confirmed she saw a patient transport plane taking off some time before. 'She just doesn't want us getting to Davy. She knows that if Davy refuted that power of attorney document . . .'

'But Davy *signed* it, Mina.' Leticia looks hopeless. 'The signature is his. I saw it myself.'

I sag back in the chair.

'Could they have faked it somehow?' Elodie asks. 'I used to copy my dad's signature with tracing paper when I wanted to bunk off school.'

'Oh God.' My stomach drops. 'I showed Olivia some of Davy's letters and papers when she brought the lilies on Monday. At one point she was taking pictures of the cottage ... She came to you the next morning with the document, didn't she?' I ask Leticia.

She nods, face pale.

Guilt drags at me. 'Then it's my fault. I gave her exactly what she needed.'

Lou offers me a biscuit. 'Don't you blame yourself, bird. You weren't to know.'

For a while, there's silence, filled only with the morose crunching of Hobnobs.

'We need to find Davy,' I tell them. 'That's the most important thing. The nurse mentioned private care. Where could she mean?'

Lou shrugs. 'Prob'ly a dozen private hospitals and nursing homes between here and Truro.'

'Penhallow won't go for any old one, though,' Elodie says, drumming her black-painted fingers on the desk. 'She's a snob. She'll want somewhere swanky.'

'Why don't you ask Sam?' Leticia says.

Elodie scowls, her face flushing red. 'She won't tell me anything. She just goes along with her sister.'

'She might.' Leticia stands, determined. 'Don't worry, Mina. We'll find him.'

By the time we emerge from Leticia's office, the light has turned purplish, already fading. One by one, the strings of Christmas lights begin to flicker on. Lou nods in approval. 'Got to decorate your place next, El. I'll bring 'em over tomorrow. Get them rigged up in time for the troyl.'

'Don't bother,' Elodie says gloomily, staring at her phone. 'We're not doing it. Can't afford to.'

'Like hell you're not. I'll bring them over at ten.'

'All right, all right.' Elodie says distractedly. 'Oh, Mina. Jem's waiting for you down by the quay. Said he had something to show you?'

Of course. It seems like a hundred years ago that we sat and drank coffee outside his cabin. 'Thanks. Are you OK?'

She just sighs. 'Yeah. I'll see you later.'

Together, we watch her walk off, hunched over her phone.

'She just doesn't want to speak to Samantha,' Lou says. 'Still awkward between them, I guess.'

'She and Sam were . . .?'

'Yup.' Lou tuts sympathetically. 'Anyone with half a brain could've seen it would never last, with the Penhallows being the way they are. Poor El still took it hard, though.'

I stare after Elodie, trying to imagine her, with her uncompromising attitude and flashing eyes and quick temper, alongside the shy, almost dreamy Sam.

'Speaking of which,' Lou slaps me on the shoulder. 'Didn't she say Fletcher was waiting for you?'

In the gathering dusk, the water of the bay is soft as feathers. Smoke hangs in the air from countless chimneys, mingling with salt, the smell of tar. At the end of the quay, a silhouetted figure stands, staring out across the waves and, for a heartbeat, he could be every sailor who ever stood, dreaming of what might wait beyond the horizon.

I step up alongside him. 'Hello,' I say self-consciously.

He looks around, his dark eyes creasing into a smile. 'Hi.'

I shiver, holding Davy's huge waterproof coat tight around myself. 'Did you hear about Davy?'

He nods. 'El told me. I can't believe they've done it. If I'd only *been* there.'

I touch his elbow gently. 'It's not your fault.'

He just shakes his head a little, before finding a crooked smile. 'Well, are you ready?'

'To go where?'

'Over to St Martin's. Like I said, there's something I think you should see.'

'Is it urgent?' I ask, rubbing at my forehead. 'Otherwise, I feel like I should be helping the others to look for Davy.'

'Lou and Leticia are already on the case. They know the area and who to ask. So does El. And Mo, with the land registry.'

I sigh, staring out over the waves. 'I still feel like I should be doing *something*.'

'This is something. And it's something Davy would want. Trust me.'

I meet his eyes, dark brown as weathered wood, and am struck by the strangeness of the fact that I *do* trust him, this person I thought the worst of only a few days ago.

'What is it?' I ask, already suspecting he won't tell me.

As I predicted, his smile turns secretive. 'You'll see.'

We take his wooden boat out across the water, but instead of steering west towards Morgelyn, we head north-east, towards St Martin's.

To my surprise, the island is bustling. Christmas lights blaze in the gathering darkness, broken into bright ripples upon the dark water, and above the noise of the engine and the slop of water, I hear music, people talking, children shrieking with laughter.

'What's going on?' I ask.

'Festive Market.'

I glance at him. '*This* is what you wanted to show me?'

'Nope.' He brings the boat alongside the jetty. Perhaps sensing my confusion, he meets my eyes. 'I'm not wasting your time, I promise. And it'll only take a few minutes.'

Hoping he's right, and hoping that *I'm* right about him this time, I climb up to the dock.

A dozen or so stalls have been set up along the quayside and are doing a roaring trade in homemade jams and cordials, liqueurs, artwork, photographs, jewellery … A brazier fills the air with the smoky scent of roasted chestnuts, while from a little café comes the irresistible waft of freshly fried doughnuts, scattered with cinnamon sugar. The fairy lights are a galaxy of rainbow stars in the darkness, even the windswept trees are merrily decorated with tinsel and ribbons, like old, hunched men getting into the spirit of the season.

My stomach growls at the scent of grilling sausages and hot, spiced wine and I realise I haven't eaten anything but biscuits all day. 'Is there time to get food?'

'Of course. After, if that's all right?'

I shoot him a searching look, but his face gives nothing away. 'OK.'

He smiles. 'This way.'

We walk through the streets until we reach a modern-looking building made from glass and wood.

ST MARTIN'S ART GALLERY, the sign says, but the place looks dark, a notice saying that it's closed for the winter. I look at Jem with a questioning frown, and he produces a ring of keys.

'Borrowed them from the gallerist earlier.'

He unlocks the door and we step inside. It's a small place, one long room with wooden floors and high exposed beams, the windows shaded by blinds. Paintings hang at regular intervals along the walls. Jem begins to flick on the lights, one after another. I turn, looking around with curiosity and confusion. Whatever I'd been expecting, it hadn't been a private tour of an island gallery. But then he beckons, pointing towards a painting at the far end of the room.

'What . . .?' I begin, stepping into the light, only for the words to fade on my lips.

My mother's face looks back at me from the painting. Her long dark hair is loose and tangled about her shoulders, garlanded with a crown of sea holly, gorse woven through the strands like yellow stars. She stands ankle deep in the surf, foam merging with her dress, beading her limbs, until I can't tell where her body ends and the sea begins. She's reaching down towards a creature: a cat as grey as dawn, with fur as soft as smoke, one paw raised to touch her outstretched fingers.

*Morgelyn ha Kath
by Davy Penhallow*

'Morgelyn and her cat,' Jem translates softly, looking up at the picture. 'It's your mother, isn't it?'

I nod, staring up at her, filled to the brim with love and sadness and joy. 'I had no idea,' I whisper.

But then, the scrap of a memory returns: my mother smiling at me in Davy's studio, candles twinkling around her, a crown of sea holly on her hair and Murr playing at her feet, batting the tendrils of a beautiful sea-blue dress. And Davy standing at the canvas, brushes in his hands, broad strokes of grey and blue and green coming alive on the surface before him.

I take a step closer to the painting. Morgelyn, Murr, Christmas, my mother, Davy's stories ... They're all connected, I realise. And standing in that pool of light, I feel something settle over me, like the warmth of a blanket on a cold night: love.

I turn to Jem, smiling through tears. 'Thank you,' I tell him.

Later, as we walk out into the festive evening, I feel a gentle heat running through my body, as if I've been lying in the sun. Despite my worry for Davy and Murr and the cottage, everything seems brighter, kinder, more possible.

Jem buys two paper cones of chestnuts, hot from the brazier, and we eat them as we wander through the festivities, burning our fingers on the scorched shells.

'Mum used to love Christmas,' I tell him. 'Her family came from Hungary, and when they were children they used to put a boot on the windowsill for Saint Nicholas to fill with candies.

So when I was kid I once put a wellington boot out, and woke up to find it filled with Quality Streets.'

Jem laughs. 'She sounds like fun.'

'She was.' I glance up at him. 'It's so strange, being back here. I keep remembering things I thought I'd forgotten. As if the memories were all locked away in a cupboard and now I'm finding them again. That probably sounds stupid.'

'Not at all. There's something special about this place. Christmas always feels different here.' He smiles wryly. 'But then, most of my childhood Christmases were spent on the move, so perhaps I feel it more.'

'You didn't grow up here?'

He shakes his head, picking another chestnut out of the bag. 'My mum, Fern, did. But she couldn't wait to leave. Sailor's blood, Gramps always says. She's a musician, met my dad on the road somewhere in Morocco or Spain. By the time she realised I was on the way, he was long gone.'

'I'm sorry.'

He shrugs. 'Don't be. I grew up touring the world with her. It was a great childhood in many ways.'

We walk along for a while, looking at the stalls, sharing the chestnuts. 'What about Elodie?' I ask.

'She's my half-sister, actually. Her dad, Yussef, is French. Mum was with him for a few years when we were living in London. Elodie went back to Paris with him when they broke up. But she came to Morgelyn the summer after our gran died to keep Gramps company and just ... never left. Mum can't understand it.'

'What about you?'

He shakes his head a little. 'I never did that well at school, got myself into all kinds of trouble. I was on a bad path, to be honest, until I met Davy when we were back here, one Christmas. He's the one who encouraged me to apply to the art summer school in Cornwall.' I remember the photograph, hanging on Davy's wall, a youthful Jem beaming out among the group. 'That turned everything around for me. When the course ended, I didn't want to go back to just drifting about the place, so he and Gramps loaned me the money to set up a studio here. I'll always be grateful to him for that.'

For a while, we don't speak. We've reached the end of the stalls and stand watching the lights glitter on the sea, the icy wind chilling our faces.

'Are you going to stay?' Jem asks. 'For Christmas, I mean,' he adds hurriedly.

I hesitate, realising that, in all the stress and worry, I haven't thought about it. But then, where else would I go? Dad and I aren't speaking, Paola's off back to Italy, and the idea of going anywhere before we've found Davy is unthinkable.

'I guess so,' I tell him. 'Anyway, I can't leave Murr alone at Christmas.'

'No,' Jem says solemnly. 'Murr takes it very seriously. She'll be expecting a traditional Christmas crab, with all the trimmings.' I let out a snort and he widens his eyes in mock-affront. 'It's not a joke! We don't do turkeys here. It's Christmas crab or nothing.'

'Yeah, right.'

'You don't believe me? Hey, Kevin?' he bellows along to a stall where a man in a striped fisherman's apron is selling cups of winkles. 'When can we have our Christmas crab?'

The man waves a spoon. 'On Christmas Eve and not a day before, Fletcher.'

Jem turns back. 'What did I say? Anyway, Murr always gets the leftovers. She'll be *very* put out if there isn't any crab.'

Together we step back among the revelry, where accordion music dances in the cold air, and faces and eyes are bright with the sea wind. I buy a batch of cinnamon doughnuts, crusting my lips and fingers with spiced sugar. Jem introduces me everywhere we go, and some smile with such familiarity that I think I must have met them before, during those few dreamlike months we lived on the islands. One woman, who is selling photographs and lino-cut prints, holds onto my hand when I shake it.

'You look just like Helena,' she says, smiling sadly.

I stare in surprise. 'You knew my mother?'

'Of course. We had work in an exhibition together once. She was a wonderful photographer. I still have one of her pieces at home.' She squeezes my fingers. 'She'd be so happy to know you've come back.'

My smile fades as we say goodbye to her.

'Are you OK?' Jem asks.

'Just thinking about Davy. That he should be here.'

He puts a hand on my shoulder. 'Don't worry, Mina. We'll get him home. I promise.'

I reach up to squeeze his hand gratefully. The moment my fingers touch his something runs through me like a current, lighting up my skin. Looking into his eyes, I see an answering expression there, a wordless question . . .

'Jem!' someone yells across the quay. I let go of his hand and he steps back, cold air rushing across my shoulder where his hand rested.

A figure is waving from the group of plastic chairs around the mulled cider stand. It's Stan from the flower farm, along with merry-looking Luis. Mr Tredugget sits beside them, his blue eyes far away, as always. 'You two young 'uns going back to Morgelyn?' he slurs.

'Luckily for you, we are.'

'Brilliant. Giz a lift?'

'Vamos!' shouts Luis, throwing back his cider.

It's a strange group that crowds onto Jem's little boat, Stan singing 'The Holly and the Ivy' at the top of his lungs, Luis trying to translate it into Spanish as we go, Mr Tredugget leaning on his cane between them, smiling quietly, me trying my best to stay upright as we scud over the waves.

'Farewell, young lovers!' Stan waves as he and Luis stagger up the path to their farm.

Together, Jem and I help Mr Tredugget onto the shore and walk him home. He lives in one of the lopsided fishermen's cottages, a stone's throw from the beach. The tiny front garden is full of driftwood and shells, sea-spurge and samphire.

'*Nos da*, Wylym,' Jem says.

'*Nos da.*' Mr Tredugget nods at me. 'She'll be here, afore long.'

'Goodnight,' I wish him, even as a shiver runs through me.

'What did he mean?' I ask Jem, as we walk away. 'Who will be here?'

'No idea. He used to be a poet, you know. He always speaks in riddles.' He stops where the sandy paths separate. 'Listen, this is probably the last thing on your mind right now but ... Ah, don't worry.'

'What is it?'

He rubs his neck, half sheepish, half rueful. 'It's just, tomorrow's Midwinter's Eve. There's always a bit of a troyl here, over at the Helm.'

'I keep hearing about this troyl.'

'Probably because it's usually the most exciting thing to happen here for months.'

I squint at him, trying to remember. 'I have a feeling we went, when I was a kid.'

Mum, dancing with someone dressed as an old-fashioned fisherman, the blue and grey dress swirling about her legs. Pipes and drums and music filling the cold, smoky air; people whooping in the strangest costumes I'd ever seen, all rags and tatters, bits of fishing net and sailcloth. A sheep's skull on a pole looming above the crowd, crowned with gorse and seaweed, but I wasn't afraid because I knew from Davy's stories that it was just the Obby Oss, the Old Grey Mare come to join the celebrations. And Davy . . . I rode high on his shoulders, so high that I could pat the Obby's head, so high that I could see the flames of the torches reflected in the sea, turning night to day on the longest night of the year . . .

'Mina?' Jem brushes my arm.

'Sorry. What were you saying?'

'I know it's not the ideal time, with everything, but I was just wondering whether . . . that is, if it even happens, whether you'd like to go to the troyl with me?'

Is this a date? I feel the heat flood into my chilled face. My brain tells me that it's wrong to be enjoying myself while the future – mine and Davy's and Murr's and the cottage's – is so uncertain, and yet, my heart whispers that this is part of something far older than all of us, that there is a power to Midwinter's Eve that cannot, should not, be ignored.

What would Davy want me to do? I ask myself. In my memories, I find the answer.

'Yes,' I tell Jem. 'I'd love to.'

CHAPTER FIFTEEN

That evening when I return, Murr seems restless, leaping down from the armchair to gallop around the house for no reason, before sitting and staring at the front door, her tail switching. Remembering the old map I saw in the museum, the strange words in old Cornish – *the place where the grey one walks* – I glance at her out of the corner of my eye, as if I might catch her in her true, magical form, only to see her mid-bath, her pink tongue sticking out, one leg raised in a very undignified manner. I laugh. She might be a strange cat, but she's a cat through and through.

I call her when I climb into bed, and she leaps onto the covers beside me, busily kneading the blanket. I'm glad of it.

As I fall asleep, the sound of the sea wind whistling around the cottage merges with my dreams, with scraps of Davy's stories about buccas and spirits and the fae folk, until I'm convinced I can hear them whispering wild words down the chimney. *They know Davy isn't here*, my dream-addled brain concludes, *they're trying to claim this place for their own.*

At one point, I wake to see Murr standing at the front door as if on guard, her tail puffed with anger. And it must be a trick of the dying fire, or my imagination, but her shadow seems so vast it fills the whole cottage. She flashes me a look, green eyes bright as new shoots, and I realise that I'm still in bed, that it's just a dream.

When I finally wake, it's to a soft tapping. *Rain*, I think, burrowing deeper under the blankets. I wait for Murr to realise I'm awake and pad across the covers to poke me with her wet nose, purring like an engine, but she doesn't. I open my eyes to see a bright beam of sunlight filtering through the porthole window, no rain at all. But still the tapping continues, echoing through the bones of the cottage. I sit bolt upright in alarm. It's coming from the front door.

Horrified, I tumble out into the main room, dragging a jumper over the pyjamas I bought in Hugh Town. Sure enough, Murr sits on the flagstones, staring fixedly at the door, her tail whipping back and forth. Before I can think about what I'm doing, I slide the bolt and wrench the door open.

A man steps back. He looks vaguely familiar in his ancient-looking waxed jacket and flat cap. He's clutching a hammer.

'What are you doing?' I demand blearily.

He grimaces. 'Sorry, Miss Kestle, I had to.'

From behind me, I hear a low growl and look down to see Murr staring with narrowed eyes. Opening her mouth, she lets out a hiss.

The man's face goes pale beneath the wind burn. 'Just a bit of paper,' he says, backing up. 'No harm done.'

Finally, I realise what he's talking about. Nailed to the front door is a laminated sign, held in place by three shiny new pins, driven into the old wood. The words are large and red and unmistakable.

PENHALLOW ESTATES: EVICTION NOTICE

'How dare you?' I snap at the man. 'This is Davy's cottage. You have no right!'

'Ms Penhallow says it's part of the estate now. She says ...' His eyes flick to Murr once again and he swallows. 'She says that you're trespassing and that if you don't leave she'll call the police.'

I remember him now, from my first night at the pub. 'Your name's Clive, isn't it?'

The man splutters something and, out of nowhere, words are on my tongue, anger filling me like storm clouds. 'May the buccas chase you. May your milk turn sour. May your nets be empty. May *she* never give you peace!'

The man stares at me in horror before turning on his heel and hurrying away up the path at a half-run. Only when he's gone does the strange feeling drain away.

'Oh God,' I groan. This place is getting to me. 'And what about you?' I demand of Murr. 'Hissing like that.'

With a strange sort of huff, she stalks off to the kitchen and starts up her demands for breakfast.

While she eats, I find a pair of pliers in one of the drawers and, as carefully as I can, prise the tacks from the door. Beneath the peeling blue paint the wood is ancient, hard as rock. No wonder it took Clive so long to hammer the pins in. Finally, the notice flaps free. I stare at it on the sandy path, imagining this door wrenched from its hinges and thrown into a skip, while someone takes a sledgehammer to the walls and a digger claws up the gorse thicket, and Murr is snatched and put into a cage, or .... It makes me feel sick.

'Not going to happen,' I tell her, stroking her back. 'I promise.'

In reply, she gently headbutts my legs.

I get to the shop half an hour later, but that's apparently enough time for the news to spread. Reni is there, along with Gryff and Mo. All of them stop talking as I walk in.

'What?' I ask.

Gryff shakes his head. 'I just had Clive banging on the door of the pub, wanting a double whisky at barely nine o'clock in the morning. White as a sheet, he was. Said you and Murr put a hex upon him.'

'That's ridiculous!'

Gryff raises an eyebrow.

'All right, I might have said some stupid things in the heat of the moment. But he deserved it.'

I pull the eviction notice from my bag and slap it on the counter.

Mo sighs when he sees it. 'Olivia's determined, we have to give her that.'

Reni tuts. 'Oh dear. Poor Clive.'

'Poor *Clive*? He works for the Penhallows!'

'So do half the people on these islands. There's not a lot of choice when it comes to work around here, trust me.' She peers at me in mock-seriousness. 'Did you really put a hex upon him?'

I snort. 'Of course not. I can't believe he took me seriously.'

But even as I say it I remember the strange feeling in my chest, the way the words seemed to come from somewhere else entirely.

Gryff rubs his chin. 'He was probably thinking of Davy's mother, Alis. She was what folk called a pellar, sort of a white witch. Ran in the family, it did, all the way backalong. Some folk wouldn't even go near the cove.'

Hair black as a guillemot's wing, eyes yellow as corn.

My skin prickles. I shrug it away. 'Any news on Davy?'

Mo nods, stirring sugar into his coffee. 'I'm waiting on a call back from a colleague who works in land preservation. And I think Lou said she had a lead? She's coming over here in a bit.'

'Thank goodness.' I stare down at the sign. 'Will Olivia really try to enforce this? Call the police?'

'She might try,' Reni shrugs. 'Whether or not they'll listen to her is another matter. Of course, Clive's brother-in-law *is* on the force ...'

I sigh. 'I guess I should apologise. Is Clive still at the pub?'

'Probably. Tread careful around my granddaughter this morning, though,' Gryff winces. 'She's in a foul temper.'

I find the pub in disarray, chairs up on tables, music blaring from a stereo as Elodie viciously scrubs the floor. She doesn't even look up when I come in. Unsurprisingly, Clive is nowhere to be seen.

'We're closed,' she snaps. Even though her face is turned away, there's no mistaking her puffy, reddened eyes.

'Elodie,' I ask. 'What's wrong?'

'Nothing.' She shoves a chair aside, sending it toppling.

I turn the stereo off. Immediately, ringing quiet fills the pub, the sound of the sea crashing outside, Elodie's own ragged breathing.

I kneel beside her on the soapy floor. 'Tell me.'

'It's everything,' she bursts, chucking the brush across the room. 'It's Davy, and the fact there's nothing we can do to save this place. The roof's falling in and we're months behind on the rent, and we've offered to try and make it up, but Olivia won't budge. We'll be homeless and jobless, and we'll have to move off the islands, away from the only home Gramps has ever known because there's no way we can afford to stay. And all because the Penhallows are greedy, selfish bastards.' She swipes her sleeve across her face.

'*Olivia* Penhallow, maybe. I'm not sure about Sam.'

Elodie's voice is biting. 'If she cared she'd do something. And it's meant to be this bloody troyl tonight, but there's no way can we hold it. We usually plan for weeks, but with Davy and the pub going under …' She sniffs. 'I've been trying to keep this place going but I just can't do it any more.'

Getting up, I grab a stack of napkins and hand them over. She wipes her eyes and for a while we just sit among the suds, with the sea wind blowing under the door. I feel like I should be scouring the country looking for Davy, but I don't know the area and even if I went to the mainland, I'd be on a wild goose chase, trying nursing homes and hospitals at random. My fingers itch to search the internet for anything that might be of use, advice on land protection orders or power of attorney, but Mo and Leticia are already the experts; all I'd be doing is telling them what they already know.

Start small, Mum always said, *one problem at a time*.

'What needs to happen, for the troyl?' I ask eventually. 'Everyone else seems to think it's going ahead.'

'They would, they don't have to host it.' Elodie blots her face. 'I don't know. There's too much to do. We'd need to get the place straightened up, get tables out of storage, make sure we have enough glasses, prep the food, replace the kegs … and I haven't even *thought* about decorations.'

I look around at the pub, its walls and shelves crammed with memorabilia, photographs going back more than a century, maps and souvenirs and gifts from visitors from all across the world. Abruptly, I stand and pull my phone from my pocket.

'What are you doing?' asks Elodie.

'Messaging Leticia. Mo said Lou was coming over here, that she had a lead on Davy. Depending on what they've found, I might have time to help.'

Elodie gets to her feet. 'Are you sure?'

'What's more use, me pacing about and worrying or lending a hand? And, anyway, what would Davy say if he hears we let Olivia Penhallow win? If we let Midwinter's Eve pass without a celebration?'

She gives me a shadow of her usual, mocking smile. 'He'd probably have Murr put a hex on me too.'

I grimace in embarrassment as a reply comes back from Leticia.

Stay where you are – over in an hour.

I show it to Elodie before rolling up my sleeves. 'So, where do I start?'

Together we clean and dust and polish, until the pub is gleaming and smells of beeswax, a fire crackling in the swept hearth. When Gryff sees what's happening, his eyes light up, and he rushes out to collar Lucas for some fresh fish.

Jem soon arrives with a box full of tools and, together, we drag some ancient picnic tables out of an old shed. We're almost finished when there's a shout from the jetty: Lou and Leticia, accompanied by a crate of ancient, rather terrifying-looking Christmas lights. Together, we crowd around the fireplace, mugs of tea in hand.

'I've called round every bloody nursing home in Cornwall,' Lou tells us, her face wind-reddened. 'And so far, nothing. But my sister's neighbour is a district nurse, and she reckons if he's still in the area, it'll be in one of five places. She's going to ask her colleagues, see if they'll spill the beans on any new admissions.'

'And if he's *not* still in the area?' I ask, nerves coiling through my stomach.

Lou just shakes her head. She doesn't need to say it.

'What else can we do?' Jem asks in frustration. 'El, you're *sure* Sam won't help?'

'I'm sure.' Elodie swallows, her expression bleak. 'I went to the house, but Olivia was there. She—' She stops talking abruptly, her voice cracking. 'Neither of them would listen to me. Olivia threatened to call the police. Now Sam won't even pick up the phone.'

It must have cost her a lot to go there, I realise.

'I'm filing an application for protected land status,' Mo says, as if trying to lift our spirits. 'All being well, it should be done by the end of the day.'

'And I've lodged a complaint with the Office of the Public Guardian,' Leticia says. 'Doing my best to get it fast-tracked.'

'Is there anything *I* can do?' I ask, feeling helpless.

Leticia lays a hand on my shoulder. 'Look after Murr, and the cottage. Keep this place alive. That's all Davy wanted from you.' Her eyes crease with an expression of pain and amusement. 'He loves the troyl. He'd be so pleased to see you here.'

My heart twists. 'He should be here, too.'

Gryff lays a hand on my other shoulder. 'He will be.'

Driven by their words, and by the need to be doing *something*, I volunteer to scrub down the tables with Jem. The sun is pale gold as elderflower wine, and by the time we're done our fingers are red and numb with cold.

At lunchtime, Gryff brings out a huge pot of winter vegetable soup. Jem and Elodie and I sit on the newly scrubbed benches, feeding crumbs to the rock pipits.

'Well, if we're going ahead tonight I'd better get the midjans and jouds out,' Jem announces, putting on a strong Cornish accent.

'The what?' I laugh.

'Midjans and jouds. Shreds and tatters. Traditional Midwinter costume.' He's sitting next to me, so close that our shoulders touch when he nudges me. 'Are you going to dress up?'

'I thought she was going as a witch,' Elodie teases.

I throw a bit of bread at her. 'I'll be going as someone who only has the clothes she bought yesterday in a charity shop in Hugh Town.'

'Have a look in Davy's wardrobe,' Jem says.

'Ha.'

'I'm serious. You might be surprised.'

'All right, you two, enough flirting. Jem, I need you down in the cellar,' Elodie says, walking away from her brother's outraged splutter.

While they get the kegs in order, I walk down to the shoreline, wanting a few minutes alone to think. Rounding the curve of the beach, I meet a familiar figure sitting among the rocks, his face turned to the sun.

'Afternoon,' I tell Mr Tredugget shyly.

He gives me a faint nod, eyes squinted tight. I can't seem to think of what else to say, so I sit on the rock next to him and close my eyes. The pale winter sunlight seeps through my eyelids, prickling my chilled skin, and soon I slip into a sort of trance, until even the chip-chirping of the rock pipits and the far-off putter of a boat's engine fades into the constant wash and lap of waves against the shore.

'Lanbenglas,' a low voice says. 'She's nearly here.'

I open my eyes to ask him what he means, only to find myself alone; nothing but the wind and the waves and the wheeling seabirds.

Rubbing a sun-chill from my arms, I make my way slowly back towards the Helm, and soon the moment is forgotten, among all the comforting chatter and activity.

With the help of a few of the island's children, I festoon the pub's porch and windowsills with seaweed and blooms of pink sea thrift, wild thyme and dried grey-blue sea holly. Jem twines fairy lights around the wind-bent trees, and when Gryff turns them on with a flourish, the whole pub comes alive, people applauding.

I smile up at the weather-beaten, ramshackle place that's the living, breathing heart of this community.

'Miss Kestle?' Gryff asks, clearing his throat. 'I was wondering . . .'

'It's Mina, Gryff. How many times—'

'Mina, then. I was wondering.' He lowers his voice. 'Are you any good with the internet? I've been having this idea. My El said it would never work but I'd say it's worth a go. Problem is, I've no idea how to do it.'

'Of course. Show me.'

With a grin, he ushers me inside.

As the afternoon wanes on the year's shortest day, the pub begins to fill with the scents of the party to come; the bright spritz of orange, the warmth of cinnamon, the pungent tang of clove, frying onions and searing meat mingling with the sharp green smell of the sea holly and ivy that decorates the beams.

Keep this place alive, Leticia said, perhaps meaning the island and the Helm both. Either way, I'm determined to do what I can to help, for all the people here, and for Davy. I plug in my phone, take Gryff's creaking old laptop into the one of the old wooden booth seats and summon up everything I learned during my short time at the agency to create the fastest campaign I ever have in my life.

Finally, as dusk falls, I call Gryff in from the kitchen.

'It's perfect,' he breathes, eyes wet at the corners. 'Oh, Miss Kestle, you're a marvel.'

At that moment Elodie walks in, her arms full of old cushions, to see us hunched over the laptop. 'Now what?' she asks, suspicious.

Gryff holds up his herb-spattered hands. 'Now, I know you

said it wouldn't work, and that folk wouldn't be interested in us, but I asked Mina and she said it was worth a shot, since it's near Christmas and all . . .'

He swivels the laptop around for her to see.

I watch in nervous silence as Elodie's eyes flicker over the screen. At the top is a picture of the pub in all its Midwinter festive glory, snapped on my phone just hours before, topped with three words.

SAVE THE HELM

'People can donate online, if they want,' I explain anxiously. 'Your granddad thought if we put it live this evening and share some photos and videos of the troyl, people might be more likely to chip in.'

For a long moment, she's silent. When she looks up, her face is caught between sadness and joy. 'You're both mad,' she says. 'But you're right. We've got nothing to lose.'

CHAPTER SIXTEEN

By the time I reach the cove, darkness is falling. In the fitful light, the cottage looks insubstantial, not wholly here. Hesitantly, I lay my palm against the cold stone wall. Each indentation, each groove means something, I realise; perhaps where someone broke this rock from the land, hundreds of years ago, where someone else shaped it into a home. This cottage stood here when Davy was born, and long before that, a witness to the unfathomable chain of chance and fate that led me here.

'Happy Midwinter,' I tell it.

A chirrup answers me and I look around to see Murr trot out of the furze, her eyes like green fire, her fur like drifting mist.

'Happy Midwinter to you, too.'

Did I ever tell you, Mina, about Midwinter's Eve? A night when the old year stumbles and the new is yet to be born, a night when time does not flow but pools, and everything that could be, is. When the piskies play their tricks and blow strange notions into human minds, when the spriggans hold their carnivals, shaking the rocks and shivering the shells on the shore until the beaches ring with their fierce music. When the buccas rush from their sea-bound caves and for one night, the sea spirits and the land spirits feast and dance on the winds until the cockerel crows . . .

'And what about Murr?' I asked.

Davy's eyes crinkled at the corners, as changeable as the sea. 'Murr has a busy night ahead of her, singing to the sea. Just as she does every year. Just as she did a thousand years ago with Morgelyn by her side.'

This place has gathered me up into its pattern, I think, as I wash in the claw-footed bath. It has taken water from my breath and hairs from my head, salt from my tears and iron from my blood and woven me into a tapestry of all the people who have gone before.

Wrapped in a blanket, I make my way into Davy's room and push aside the curtain that hides the alcove wardrobe.

You might be surprised, Jem said, and, sure enough, as soon as I start to brush through the clothes I feel cool silk beneath my fingers, hear the clatter of beads and pull the garment free.

It's a gown of ice blue and sea-holly green and smoke grey, made from long tatters of silky fabric that tangle together, sewn all over with glass beads, like flecks of ice. It's the dress my mother wore when she posed as Morgelyn, I realise. And it's still here, as carefully kept as if she had just hung it up.

Hesitantly, I let the dress fall over my head. The silk whispers against my skin, the beads like droplets of cold water on my face. The faintest ghost of her perfume still clings to the fabric, and for a moment, my heart crushes in my chest with how much I miss her. The dress is tighter on me than it was on her, coming up short at the ankle, but when I turn to the mirror, and blur my eyes, I almost see her face.

'What do you think?' I whisper, staring at the image in the little age-spotted mirror. And for a moment, I feel her with me, her smile, her hand against my cheek.

You look lovely, Mina.

Murr lets out a soft meow, half-chirrup, as if in agreement. As she bats at the trailing ribbons of the dress I reach down towards her, just as my mother did in the painting. Murr looks up at me, and then does something I've never seen before. She raises herself on her back legs and reaches up one soft paw to touch my fingers.

I look into her bright green eyes and, for a heartbeat, less, it's as if I'm surrounded by the violent roar of the winter sea, grey waves swamping everything save for a single golden light on the horizon. A light that is life, that is hope. Then, Murr rears up and headbutts my palm before running off into the kitchen, telling me it's time for supper.

Blinking hard, I follow her out.

While she eats, I fill every saucer I can find with milk and place them about the house.

'For the sea spirits,' I tell Murr. 'Don't go drinking them all yourself.'

She simply gives me a blink, slow and regal, and for a moment I think I see someone else, some*thing* else, looking back at me from her sea-green eyes; something calm and knowing and very, very old.

She leaves me as always where the cove meets the path, watching me for a moment before disappearing into the gorse, into the private twisting paths that only she and the rodents and lizards and beetles know. Gathering my courage, I carry on alone, breath misting in the freezing air, nerves and excitement coiling in my stomach.

I crest the headland to find an island transformed.

Lights blaze all along the shore, lanterns and braziers reflected in the dark waves like scattered gold. Music drifts on the air, drums like the heartbeat of some great creature, pipes that could be the cries of sea birds, hands clapping like oars slapping water, voices raised in shouts. It's a clear, crisp winter night, the stars blazing above and I breathe in deep, woodsmoke scratching my nostrils along with wet sand, sweet, hot apples, meat roasted over flames . . .

Crunching down the sandy path, I'm stunned by how many people there are. I'd expected maybe a dozen, but there must be over a hundred. The tiny harbour is crowded with boats and skiffs, jostling for space alongside the jetty. Almost everyone is in costume and, for a moment, I feel as if I've slipped across a border into another world. There are masks of feathers and fish scales, nets and weeds. I see threadbare ballgowns and fraying dinner jackets alongside frock coats and rubbery waders, all of them tattered and torn, like my own dress, as if the people here have been feasting and drinking for centuries, not hours.

A night when the old year stumbles and the new is yet to be born . . .

'Mina!' Elodie waves from outside the pub, where they've set up the huge pot of mulled cider. She wears a collar made from shimmering black feathers, black eyeliner thick across her eyes, plumes stuck among her dark curling hair. 'Where's the costume?' she grins.

Self-consciously, I shrug off Davy's huge old coat. The cold air prickles my skin, lantern light catching on the glass beads.

'I found it in Davy's wardrobe,' I tell her, face growing hot. 'Do you think it's OK that I'm wearing it?'

'I think he'd be honoured.' She hands me a glass of hot cider. *'Yeghes da.'*

'Yeghes da.'

Even if I can't recognise faces, I begin to see familiar figures, hear familiar voices among the crowd. Gryff is unmistakable in his wig of seaweed and bottletops and a gold ballgown from the 1980s. Mo too in a satin smoking jacket and plain black eye mask, like Zorro. Stan and Luis appear dressed as Regency dandies, to great applause. Finally, I spot Lou and Leticia, eating crab on one of the benches, and weave my way towards them.

'Mina!' Leticia's eyes are kind behind a mask that looks as

if it was made by one of her children, sea flowers stuck in her wayward hair. 'You look wonderful.'

'It's true,' Lou adds. 'Davy would be made up to see you here.'

My cheeks, already growing hot from the chill air and cider, redden further. 'Thanks. I don't suppose there's any news yet?'

'Not yet,' Lou says, waving a crab leg at me. 'But I think we're getting close.'

'You'll let me know as soon as you hear anything?'

'Of course,' Leticia promises, squeezing my hand. 'Now go on, enjoy yourself. Davy wouldn't want you to be sad, not tonight. And anyway,' she smiles. 'I think someone might be waiting for you.'

Beside one of the braziers, a tall figure stands, wearing a coat of tattered black and grey cloth that merges with the shadows. Dead twigs and bits of flotsam crown his hat in a mockery of fresh flowers, dark make-up is streaked across his eyes.

'Jem!' I laugh.

He gives a mock little bow. 'Mina, you look—'

'Just like her. I know.'

'No,' he smiles. 'You look beautiful. Like yourself.'

The firelight flickers across his skin, shadows merging with those that spread beneath his eyes. I hold his gaze and my whole body seems to thrum with possibility, with the heat of him, the desire to feel his hand on my waist, my cheek . . .

'Here,' he says, moving forwards. 'This is for you.'

It's all I can do to tear my eyes from his. Something glitters in his hands. It's a necklace, made from thin strands of silver wire, interwoven with pieces of sea glass – bottle green and smoky grey and pearly white – all tumbled by the sea into smoothness, washed up here from the corners of the world and fashioned into something beautiful.

'Did you make this?' I ask, turning it in the light.

He smiles sheepishly. 'You don't have to wear it. I just thought—'

'I love it.'

My hand touches his and there's no denying it; the charge that leaps between us, that shoots through me like a firework and draws us together. I lift the necklace and drape it around my neck. The droplets are cold as seawater against my skin, making me shiver, even more so when Jem's warm fingers brush the nape of my neck as he secures the clasp and gently touches my shoulder.

'Miss Mina!' a voice yells, and I look up, my face hot. Stan stumbles across from the dancefloor, mopping his face with a handkerchief. 'May I have this dance?'

I glance back to Jem, wanting him to step close again, to take my hand and lead me somewhere else. 'I don't know the steps,' I say vaguely.

'Doesn't matter,' Stan declares, taking my elbow. 'There en't any!'

Jem laughs when I give him a comically pleading look, but there's nothing I can do to avoid being dragged into the dance. At least Stan's right about one thing; there don't seem to be any steps at all. Everyone makes up their own, galloping here and there, spinning and kicking until we're enveloped in a cloud of sand and smoke and laughter. When the song ends and the musicians pause for breath, I disentangle myself from Stan's be-ribboned coat and escape into the pub before they start up again.

It's crowded in here, a fire blazing, faces shiny with warmth. There's no sign of Jem, but Elodie waves from the counter.

'Mina, come look!'

I squeeze through the crowd at the bar, all gathered around Gryff's laptop. The fundraiser is live on the screen and when I see the donation bar, my mouth falls open. 'We're already past the initial target,' Elodie says. 'I can't believe it!'

I return her wild hug, laughing as I see Paola's name ping up among the donors, followed by other friends in London who I sent the link to, followed by neighbours, acquaintances, strangers from around the world, all sharing, all giving what they can to keep this little pub alive at Christmas.

The loud *pop* of a champagne cork fills the air. '*Montol lowen!*' Gryff cries, and then Jem is beside me again, his clothes smelling of icy sea air and smoke, his hand lingering on mine as he hands me a glass of champagne.

One glass becomes two, becomes cider and talking and laughing with Jem and Lucas and their friends from other islands around a campfire, Jem's knee pressed to mine, a blanket shielding our shoulders from the cold. As the night deepens, the atmosphere grows more raucous, the music faster, people shouting themselves hoarse in celebration. Finally, when a wild tune starts up, I can't wait any more and I take Jem's hand, dragging him with me into the dance.

His arm goes around my waist, fingers tangled with mine as we spin and gallop to the feverish music, played on wood and bone and gut, until other people become insubstantial, their clothes disintegrating into shadow and sea foam. I spin and from the corner of my eye, I think I see someone in a dress like mine, dancing with a man whose hair is silver-streaked sand, his eyes like the sky. But they're lost in an instant and so am I, becoming limbs moving to music, which is also the crash of waves and the roar of wind and constant, undying song of the sea.

I stumble and someone catches me. Jem. Jem, whose heart I can feel beneath my palm, as fast as the drums, whose body is pressed against mine in the shadows at the edge of the dance.

We meet eyes for one breathless second and then his mouth is on mine, and I kiss him fiercely, tasting smoke and liquor and the sweetness of winter apples.

'Come home with me?' he breaks away long enough to ask and *yes*, I reply, *yes*, because there's nothing I want more, on this night when the old world is ending and anything can happen.

'My coat,' I whisper, lips tingling, body thrilling.

'Where is it?'

'The pub.'

'I'll get it.' He leaves me with a last kiss, before striding off towards the back of the Helm.

I take a deep breath of the cold marine air, feeling as light as sea foam, as alive as lightning across the sea. Tipping back my head to look at the stars, I think I see a flash in the darkness where the gorse meets the sand: the eyeshine of an animal, looking my way.

'Murr?' I frown and take a few unsteady steps towards the path that leads to Davy's cottage. I've never seen her this far away from the cove.

Just as I think I've imagined it, I see them again: silver eyes, disappearing into shadow. 'Murr!' I call, following.

I stumble up the narrow path, flame-blind in the darkness, guided only by starlight until, abruptly, I see a glow, pinkish-orange. The sun rising already? But it can't be: this is Midwinter's Eve, the longest night of the year. The sun won't rise for hours yet.

Then the smell of smoke catches in my nose, thicker and more ragged than any bonfire and with a terrible, crushing realisation I break into a run, slipping and crawling up the crest of the hill and onto the headland.

A cry escapes me when I see the horror below. The furze all around Davy's cottage is ablaze, dead bracken sparking and springing into flame, acrid smoke filling the air. I catch one flash of movement among the gorse, the whisk of a small grey body, running in fright.

'Murr!' I yell, tripping forwards and for a second she turns towards me, before a branch falls flaming into her path.

With a scream, I throw myself towards the gorse, but the heat is intense and all too soon I can't breathe, can't see, my eyes streaming and stinging.

I force them open and, for an instant, I think I catch a glimpse of something on the dark waves, pale as a ghost; a boat speeding away from the cove.

Then, the vision is gone, smoke billowing, and there's nothing I can do but stumble onto the path, shrieking for help over the ravenous, consuming roar of the flames.

'You're lucky you saw it when you did,' Lou tells me, her face haggard and soot-streaked in the grey light of dawn. 'Or it could've been far worse.'

'It was Murr,' I croak. 'She came to find me, to warn me.' I blink burning eyes, looking around at the destruction.

A great scar of blackened heather and gorse spreads in a ring around the cottage, still smoking in places. Davy's studio is destroyed, glass shattered, stones slicked black with water and smoke, but miraculously, the rest of the cottage is undamaged.

'As if it were protected or something,' Elodie murmurs, handing me a bottle of water. I drink, soothing my seared throat.

Lou's right, it could have been worse, I tell myself dully. If it hadn't been the night of the festival, if so many people hadn't come running at once to form a chain, passing buckets of seawater and spades full of sand to douse the flames, who knows how much more would have been lost?

But as it is, so much has been. *Look after Murr*, Leticia had said. *That's all Davy wanted from you*. I squeeze my eyes closed, wracked by the thought that I've failed him and Murr both, when it mattered.

'Has anyone seen Murr?' I ask for the twentieth time.

Faces look back at me without speaking, exhausted and filthy. I've searched everywhere, in every corner of the house, down by the shoreline, even among the charred remains of the gorse and heather.

'She'll be back,' Jem says gently, pulling his jacket up around my shoulders. 'She was probably just scared and is hiding somewhere, that's all. She's clever, remember?'

I nod, resting my head against his shoulder, but I can't ignore the gnawing fear in my stomach as I remember Leticia's words about the guardianship, about Davy's estate passing to whoever held it in the event of Murr's death. And even if the guardianship is superseded by the power of attorney, what if someone was trying to make sure . . .?

Outside the Helm, the ground is strewn with the remains of the celebration. We sag onto the benches in the chill smoky air, still in ruined costumes, like revellers from the longest party there has ever been.

Any night but Midwinter, and it wouldn't have happened, I can't help but think. *Any night but the one where the walls between the worlds are thin.*

'Mina?' Jem pushes a mug of coffee in front of me. 'You're sure you're OK? You breathed a lot of smoke.'

I nod, rubbing at my pounding head. 'I'll be fine.'

'Here.' Gryff plonks down a tray. 'Bacon sarnies. And veggie for the non-meat eaters. Got to keep up your strength.'

Gratefully, I take one, and for a while, we just sit in silence as a new day breaks, taking comfort in the familiar taste of fresh bread and melted butter.

'It wouldn't have happened if Davy had been here,' I say at last.

Gryff's voice is gentle. 'It was an accident. Could have been anything.'

'A stray spark from one of the torches, perhaps,' Mo says, hands wrapped around his coffee. 'Or a cigarette butt?'

'No.' I sit back. 'It was deliberate.'

'We don't know that.'

Jem shakes his head. 'I think Mina's right. I'm sure I smelled petrol. And the way the gorse burned, in an almost perfect ring around the cottage ...'

We all look at each other.

'No,' Gryff shakes his head. 'Surely not.'

Elodie laughs humourlessly. 'Wouldn't put it past her.'

'Did you see *anything* else, Mina?' Mo asks.

In that moment I remember the ghostly boat I'm sure I glimpsed through the smoke. What better way to clear people from the land, to be rid of an inconvenient animal at the same time? What better way to get what she wants?

'I didn't see anyone,' I tell them softly. 'But whatever's going on here, it stops. Now.'

Later, Jem takes me over to St Mary's. It's a blustery day, a freezing wind blowing, the sun veiled behind thick clouds, as if it too has reason to hide its face after the night's events. Both of us are quiet as Hugh Town comes into view, Penhallow House standing proud on the hill.

'Sure you don't want me to come?' Jem asks, his dark eyes narrowed as he navigates towards the quay.

'No,' I tell him. 'But thanks.'

He brushes a strand of my hair from my forehead, still wet from showering in the Helm's poky bathroom. 'I'll check in with Leticia and wait for you there.'

News of the fire has already spread across the islands. The moment I step onto the quay, and all through the town, people hurry over to ask if I'm all right, to ask for news of Davy, of Morgelyn, of Murr. Some I recognise – Lucas's friends from the party, the woman who sold photographs at the market, Kevin the fishmonger – but others I don't. It doesn't seem to matter that I've never spoken to many of them before; they clasp my arm, call me 'bird' and 'love', their faces full of concern. I get asked to at least three houses for Christmas dinner, another two for Christmas Eve, and my eyes sting with gratitude.

But finally, I have to leave the main streets and walk through the gate of Penhallow House. This time, the door is closed, no Philip lounging on the sun-lit step, no scents of coffee or breakfast. Nerves rush through me as I ring the doorbell, but the memory of Murr's bright eyes, turned towards mine a moment before she disappeared into the heart of the fire, turns me to stone.

The door opens after several rings. Sam stands there in a dressing gown, looking pale and nauseous.

'Mina.' She takes a step back. 'What are you doing here?'

She knows something, I realise. Her usual dreamy expression is gone, replaced by discomfort.

'What do you think?' I say, shoving past her. 'Where is she?'

She follows as I stride towards the study. 'Mina, is everything OK? What happened last night? I saw the smoke . . .'

Ignoring her, I push open the door and step inside.

Olivia stands behind the desk. She looks tired, not her usual coiffed self, bags beneath her eyes.

'Mina. Glad to see you're OK.' Her eyes dart to Sam. 'We heard about the fire.'

I only stare at her. In that moment, I wish that Davy's stories of white witches and ill-wishes were true and that I could curse Olivia Penhallow, put a hex on her for life.

'This stops,' I tell her. 'Now.'

'What stops?' Her grey eyes flash. 'You mean the plans for Morgelyn? Mina, you have to understand, this isn't personal. I have a responsibility to do what's best for the estate—'

'What's financially best for *you*, you mean.' My voice is bitter, still raw from the smoke. Leaning forward, I place my hands on the desk. 'Or is burning down an old man's home before Christmas and killing his cat your way of doing business?'

Her face turns bloodless, lips tight. 'Be careful,' she snaps. 'That's a serious allegation.'

'Mina.' Sam steps alongside us. 'Livvy had nothing to do with the fire.'

I don't take my gaze from Olivia's. 'I saw you. I saw your boat. People could have died.'

She scoffs. 'That's utterly untrue.'

'Then it won't worry you when I say that after I leave here, I'm going straight to the police, to report it alongside the fraud you've already committed.'

Olivia opens her mouth, face twisted.

'Stop!' Sam steps between us. 'Please, I know things have been difficult with Davy, but we've always had his best interests in mind. And Mina, I'm sorry, but he really did sign the cottage over to Livvy himself. I've seen the papers.'

I glance at her desperate face. 'Then check your sister's phone. She took a photo of Davy's signature the day before she produced that power of attorney document.'

Olivia only stares at me, jaw ticking. Her phone lies on the desk before her.

'Go on,' I tell her. 'Let Sam look, if you have nothing to hide.'

She snatches up the phone, drops it into her pocket. 'I don't need to. She's my sister. She believes me. As will the police.' But beneath the utter confidence in her voice, I think I hear something: a hairline crack of fear. 'You have no proof of anything. Now, I'd suggest you get out of my house before I report you for trespassing. And, rest assured, you'll be hearing from my solicitor.'

With one last look at her pallid face, I turn on my heel and march out of the room, flinging a glance at the portrait of Davy's father before I go. No wonder he got away from all this. I slam the front door so hard that the wreath showers holly berries onto the mat.

I'm halfway down the path when I hear it open again behind me.

'Mina!' Sam calls quietly, as if afraid of being overheard. I ignore her, striding towards the gate. I hear bare feet on the stones as she runs after me.

'Mina, wait,' she says, catching at my arm.

'What?' I snap, tugging it out of her grip.

'You've got this all wrong—'

'Don't pretend you care.' My breath mists in the air as I let out a bitter laugh. 'Elodie was right. You do whatever Olivia says.'

At the mention of Elodie's name, Sam's cheeks turn pink. 'I don't . . .' She trails off. When she looks back at me, there are tears in her eyes. 'Autumn Grove,' she says quietly.

'What?'

She raises her chin in something like defiance. 'Autumn Grove Private Residential Care Home. That's what it's called. That's where Davy is.'

CHAPTER SEVENTEEN

'Jem,' I yell into my phone. 'I know where he is! Tell Elodie, tell everyone!'

The island grapevine does its work at triple-fast speed, and by the time I stagger breathless onto the road that leads to the air terminal, I hear a frantic honking behind me. It's Leticia.

'Why isn't Jem with you?' I ask.

'He's gone to find El,' she says, red-cheeked. 'Get in. No time to lose!'

In her little car we whine up the rest of the hill, screeching into the car park. The terminal seems busy, comparatively, a couple of tourists and the local vicar waiting with their luggage beside Lou, who suppresses a belch, looking decidedly worse for wear.

'We've found Davy!' I yell, charging through the doors.

Lou gapes at me for a moment, before unceremoniously thrusting the vicar's suitcase back into his hands. 'Sorry, Alan, sorry, you two,' she says to the tourists. 'This flight is now delayed.'

'Now wait a tick—' the vicar protests.

'Ask at the counter, they'll sort you out.' Lou zips her jacket up to the chin. 'Let's go.'

We dash across the runway towards the plane. 'It's a place called Autumn Grove,' I tell them, over the wind coming in from the sea. 'I've looked it up, it's a private nursing home near Marazion. I called but they wouldn't tell me anything.'

'No wonder,' Leticia pants. 'I've heard of that place. It's where the rich send their elderly relatives. Very exclusive.'

'Don't worry.' Lou crams her pilot's hat onto her head. 'I'll have you there in record time.'

Just as I'm about to tell her to wait, I see two figures duck beneath the wire fence at the edge of the runway and start to sprint across the grass. Jem and Elodie.

'Come on!' Leticia says, holding down a hand to help them aboard.

They collapse into the plane's seats, sweating and cursing.

'No way . . .' Elodie gasps, 'going . . . without us.'

I grip Jem's hand as, with a whoop, Lou starts the engines.

AUTUMN GROVE, the discreet sign reads, PRIVATE RESIDEN-TIAL ESTABLISHMENT.

Beyond imposing gates, I get a glimpse of what might have once been a manor house at the end of a long drive. High brick walls stretch off into the woodland that surrounds the place.

'What is this, a nursing home or a prison?' Lou swears, rattling the locked gate.

I jam my thumb to the intercom button.

'Hello,' I call when it crackles into life. 'We're here to see one of your residents, a Mr Davy Penhallow?' I look around at the others, holding my breath.

'Do you have an appointment?' a cool voice answers.

'No, we don't. But I'm his goddaughter, and I'm with his friends. I'm sure he'd be pleased to see us.'

'One moment.'

The intercom goes dead. A red light winks and I realise we're being watched by the beady eye of a camera above the gate. Seconds later, the intercom buzzes back to life.

'I'm sorry but Mr Penhallow is not accepting visitors right now.'

'So you've spoken to him?' I demand. 'He told you that?'

'It's here on his notes. No visitors.'

I grit my teeth. *Olivia.* 'Well, then can I speak to someone there about his condition? A doctor?'

'Are you next of kin?'

I stare up into the camera's cold gaze. 'I told you, I'm his goddaughter.'

A nasal sigh. 'I'm afraid that's not quite the same thing.'

'Look, his family are keeping him here against his will,' Elodie snaps, barging in next to me. 'He shouldn't even *be* here, he would never have agreed to come of his own volition.'

'Madam, if you raise your voice again, I will call security. I'll have to ask you all to leave now and stop blocking the entrance.'

'Wait!'

The intercom clicks into silence. With a curse Elodie slams a Doc Marten into the gate, setting an alarm off.

Hurriedly, we pile back into the Isles of Scilly Travel minibus and reverse down the drive, out of sight.

'We have to get in there somehow,' I say, turning in my seat.

'We could ram the gates,' Lou says darkly.

'Or climb over the wall?' Jem ventures.

I stare at the long drive ahead, and for the first time I find myself wondering: what would Olivia Penhallow do? It comes to me immediately, so fast that I almost laugh.

'What are you doing?' Jem asks, as I pull out my phone, calling Autumn Grove once again.

I hold my finger to my lips as it rings, as the same nasal, bored voice answers.

'Oh, hello,' I greet, in my best clipped British accent, channelling Olivia, channelling every client who ever looked straight over my head at the agency. 'Olivia Penhallow here, calling about my cousin ...'

Half an hour later I stand outside the gates once again, clutching a folder of papers from Leticia's handbag. My hair's twisted into a tight bun, and I'm wearing Elodie's coat and a huge pair of Lou's driving glasses; as much of a disguise as we could scrape together from whatever was lying around in the van.

I'm sending a solicitor along with some papers for Mr Penhallow to sign, I'd told the home, doing my best Olivia impression. *A Mrs Strout. She should be there within the hour.*

Please, I think, as Leticia rings the intercom and gives her name. *Please have bought it.*

I glance at Leticia out of the corner of my eye. Her lips are set into a sort of grimace, her hands trembling. She isn't built for espionage. Then, just as she looks at me in panic, the lock buzzes and the gates slowly drift open.

'Just breathe,' I tell her out of the corner of my mouth as we walk up the driveway.

From the outside, Autumn Grove looks grand; frost-rimed benches on the gravel paths and a prim rose garden, cut right back for winter. But then I hear the way the gate clangs shut behind us, see the reinforced doors, the alarms, the sterile-looking blinds on the windows.

Leticia evidently does too, because her mouth firms and by the time we walk up the front steps and into the overly warm reception area, she seems an entirely different person.

'Mrs Strout,' she announces loudly to the receptionist. 'To see Mr Penhallow.'

'Yes, we're expecting you,' says a young man with a neatly trimmed moustache. 'Your identification, please?'

She slaps her driving licence onto the counter. 'My assistant.' She waves a dismissive hand at me. 'Here to carry the documents.'

I keep my head ducked meekly.

'Very good,' the receptionist oozes. 'Mr Penhallow is in room twenty-three of our East Wing.'

'How is he?' Leticia asks, momentarily slipping out of character. 'I mean,' she corrects. 'Is he lucid enough to sign papers, as Ms Penhallow said?'

'He should be, yes. I believe he is on a course of sedatives. If you wait a moment, I'll ask a nurse to—'

'No need,' Leticia trills. 'We're on a tight schedule. Christmas, you know.' She clicks her fingers at me and marches away from the reception, down a hallway with EAST above the door.

'Sedatives?' I hiss as we hurry along, rage and guilt squirming in my stomach.

Leticia's lips are pressed white with anger, eyes fixed ahead. 'We have to be fast. I don't think he likes us being here without a nurse.'

The corridor seems endless, a thick burgundy carpet hushing our steps. The air smells strangely stale, of old meals and cleaning products and hot radiators. From somewhere, a TV warbles loudly with the sounds of a daytime game show. We hurry past what looks like a lounge, counting the doors. Nineteen, twenty, twenty-one . . .

We stop. On the door of room twenty-three, a gold engraved name plaque reads D. PENHALLOW. The sight of it – so permanent looking – chills me.

'Go ahead,' Leticia whispers. 'I'll keep watch.'

Shaking, I push open the door.

The room beyond is small, papered in a faded floral print. The curtains are closed tightly, even though it's past noon, the whole atmosphere thick and airless.

'Davy?' I blink in the gloom. 'I'm here.'

There's no response. As my eyes adjust, I see a huddled shape in a hospital-style bed, head pressed into the pillow, a deep frown between his brows. Around him, the sheets are tangled, as if he has been tossing and turning in his sleep. 'Davy?' I murmur, creeping closer. 'Please, wake up.'

I reach out and take his worn hand, holding it in both of mine. He stirs, eyes flickering groggily to focus on my face. For a long moment, he doesn't speak.

'Helena?' he finally croaks, voice thick and slurred.

My mother's name. Heart aching, I turn on the bedside light. 'No, it's me. It's Mina.'

His hand tightens on mine, his eyes narrow in the light and for the first time in twenty years, my godfather meets my gaze.

'Mina?' he breathes. His face looks lopsided, mouth drooping, but still I smile for joy, my eyes stinging.

'Long time no see.'

His rheumy eyes fill, tears running down his weathered cheeks as he holds my hand tight.

'Don't cry,' I tell him. 'Davy, it's all right, don't cry.'

'You ...' His voice is laboured. 'You came.'

'Of course I did,' I laugh, blinking away tears. 'No thanks to your mysterious note.'

'Thought ...' He works his mouth. 'Thought I was ... dying. Thought ... too late.' Concern creases his face. 'M–Murr?'

I can't lie to him, not now. 'There was a fire. Murr ran off. I don't know where she is ...' I can't go on. Davy just closes his eyes, as if in pain.

The door creaks and Leticia slips into the room. 'Mina, there's a nurse coming with a trolley.' She looks at Davy, her face collapsing into relief and pity and happiness. 'Oh, Davy.'

'T–tish?' Davy breathes, and he seems so confused, so woozy. *Sedatives*, I remember with a burst of rage.

'We're here to get you out,' I say, urging him to sit up. 'Can you stand?'

Holding onto my hand, he hauls himself up to sitting, but his left hand doesn't seem to be working and I know even before he puts his feet on the floor that he won't be able to make it more than a few steps. 'Here!' Leticia says, seizing a wheelchair from the corner of the room.

I help him into the chair and grab a blanket from the bed to tuck over his pyjamas.

'Mina.' He tries to catch at me as I fuss. There's so much in his gaze; sadness, desperation, confusion. 'Mina. Tell . . .'

I squeeze his hand. 'I know, Davy. I found the letters you tried to send me. I'm so sorry, I had no idea.'

He shakes his head, fighting to form the words he wants to say.

A knock on the door makes us all freeze. 'Mr Penhallow,' a cheery voice rings. 'Time for your lunchtime medication.'

With a nod at me, Leticia opens the door an inch, blocking the nurse's view.

'Excuse me,' she snaps, 'we're in the middle of a very important legal consultation.'

I can't see the nurse, but I hear her momentary stunned silence. 'Well, I'm afraid I have to give Mr Penhallow his prescribed—'

'Please return in five minutes. We'll be finished by then.'

She slams the door, one hand going to her mouth, and after a horribly long pause, I hear the squeak of the trolley, continuing away down the hall.

'What do we do?' Leticia hisses. 'We'll never get past reception.'

'Lounge.' Davy says groggily.

With a nod at me, Leticia creaks open the door and I push Davy out in the chair. It isn't far to the lounge, perhaps twenty feet, but with every squeak of the wheel, every hurried footstep my heart begins to beat harder, until I can barely breathe.

We barge into a room stuffed with squashy armchairs, where a television is turned up loud. A few older people stare at us as we enter, but I ignore them, weaving with Davy in his chair past tables and footstools towards a huge pair of French windows.

'I say . . .' one old man challenges as Leticia rattles the handle, but his voice is lost in the shrilling of an alarm as, with a final shove, she presses down on a bar and the doors burst open.

'Hold on, Davy,' I yell, as we race down a ramp and onto a patio. It's only a dozen paces to the main drive, two dozen more to the gates.

'Hurry!' Leticia calls, and I hear a commotion in the room behind us, but I don't look back; I push the chair as fast as I can across the gardens, down onto the slick tarmac of the drive, Davy's white hair blowing in the wind as we go.

'The gates,' I gasp, realising that we'll be trapped, only to see something shoved between them, preventing them from closing: one of Elodie's boots. A blur of white appears at the end of the drive. It's the minivan, reversing rapidly towards us with its back doors open, Jem and Elodie crouched just inside.

'Come on!' Jem yells.

Leticia charges on ahead, pulling the gates open and, a few seconds later, I squeeze Davy and the chair through. Elodie and Jem are waiting, taking hold of a side of the chair each, and together, we lift Davy up into the van.

'Go!' Leticia shrieks, slamming the back doors and racing around towards the passenger seat. 'Go, go, go!'

Behind her, the receptionist is running for the gates, followed by two uniformed security personnel. I get one glimpse of their livid faces before Lou takes off in a squeal of tyres and a burst of exhaust.

'Suckers!' she crows.

I turn to Davy, grinning, only to realise he's gasping for

breath. Abruptly, I'm terrified that we've done the wrong thing; that it's all been too much. But when I take his hand I see that his eyes are bright, his mouth curved lopsidedly into a ghost of his old, knowing smile as he starts to laugh.

CHAPTER EIGHTEEN

'Physically, there's damage from the stroke he's suffered,' Doctor Osman says quietly as we stand in the doorway of the cottage. 'The movement on his left side has been affected, as well as his speech, as you've probably seen.'

'Will he recover?' The idea that Davy might lose his storyteller's voice, his use of a paintbrush and pencil fills me with sadness.

'Many people make very good recoveries,' Doctor Osman assures me. 'But it depends on the individual. These first few weeks are critical. A course of sedatives are not something I would have recommended.'

A wave of anger at Olivia Penhallow courses through me. Jem squeezes my shoulder.

'Is there anything we can do?' he asks.

The doctor looks between us, her brown eyes serious. 'Help him practise movement and speech. The medication the hospital prescribed should prevent any further attacks.' She pauses. 'Your godfather is a determined man, Miss Kestle. I have every hope he'll recover, especially in his own home, but you must prepare yourself for the fact he might not. It's a matter of will, as much as anything.'

I want to disagree, to argue childishly that now Davy is back everything is going to be OK. But I know that might not be true. Although the cottage has been cleaned and aired, the studio is still ruined, patched up with sailcloth. Olivia Penhallow still has the legal documents. Worst of all, Murr is still missing.

I force myself to nod.

Doctor Osman smiles reassuringly. 'I'll have the district nurse add him to the rounds. But for now, rest is what he needs.'

We watch her go, picking her way through the blackened heather. All around the cottage, right down to the shore, bowls of potted shrimp – Murr's favourite – remain untouched.

'Where is she?' I ask Jem.

Wordlessly, he pulls me close. I lean against him, and for a while we just stand like that, out in the cold, watching the gathering dusk.

'I'll go and look for her in the dunes again,' he says finally. 'Unless you want me to stay here?'

I look up at him, smiling wearily. 'We'll be fine.'

'You told me you'd bring him home. And you did.'

'*We* did. I only wish . . .'

He puts a hand to my cheek. 'Murr will be back. You'll see.'

After a heartbeat's hesitation, he leans down towards me. His lips are warm against mine, and I hold him tightly, fingers tangling in the curls at the nape of his neck. At last, he steps away.

'If I don't go now, I never will,' he says. 'But I'll be back tomorrow, first thing.'

'And you'll let me know if you find . . .?' I can't bring myself to say it, let alone think it.

He squeezes my hand. 'I'll let you know.'

I watch him crunch up the path over the headland until, with a final wave, he disappears into the blackened heather.

Sighing, I close the door on the coming night and lean against it, the long day replaying behind my eyelids: the plane journey back to the islands, Davy resting against me, wrapped in blankets; the journey down to the quay, where Gryff and Lucas and almost every boat from Morgelyn seemed to be waiting; the hero's welcome when we finally lifted Davy onto the shore in his chair, people whooping and clapping, Davy shyly raising a trembling hand in thanks; his face, when he saw the blackened heather and gorse; the tears that fell as he touched the charred branches.

With a sigh, I creep to the bedroom and peek through the door. He's asleep between clean, worn sheets. The light from the oil lamp is low, golden and someone – Jem, maybe? – has placed a vase of winter wildflowers on the windowsill; spiky sea holly and gleaming buckthorn berries and sprigs of living gorse, filling the room with their bright scent.

Davy stirs, reaching out a hand across the blankets to the spot where a warm, soft bundle of grey fur would usually sleep, purring through the night.

'Murr?' he calls weakly.

I go to him, taking his hand. 'She's not here.'

Blinking, he focuses on me, and a sleepy smile crosses his face that clearly says, *But you are.*

'I'm so sorry,' I tell him for the hundredth time. 'If I'd been here that night, if I'd kept better watch ...'

He moves his head back and forth on the pillow. 'Change,' he murmurs, before looking towards the window. 'Old year end ... ending.'

'And Christmas Eve in two days,' I say, trying to find something joyful. 'If you don't mind, I'd like to spend it here with you.' He doesn't answer, closing his eyes. 'Davy?'

Slowly, he disentangles his hand from mine, and points towards the alcove wardrobe with its painted sailcloth.

'The letters?' I ask. 'I know. I told you, I found them all. Well, Murr found them, chasing a spider.'

But Davy shakes his head, gesturing again more forcefully, and so I go to pull back the curtain, staring at the hanging garments.

'What is it? I don't see anything.'

Davy gestures. *Up.*

Frowning, I stand on tiptoe to peer onto the shelf where the hatbox full of letters once sat. There's something else there, I realise, an object wrapped in cloth. Reaching up, I drag it towards me, into the light. Frowning, I turn to Davy and he nods, closing his eyes.

The moment I pull the fabric away, I realise what it is. Mum's photograph, the one she gave Davy that Christmas.

In my memory it was a hazy, summer scene, but now I see that it's so much more. It shows the cottage and the cove at the moment of a glorious, midsummer sunset. The light is thick as honey, turning the petals of the wildflowers and the tips of the long seagrass into glowing candles. A small shape sits on the front step of the cottage, shadow stretching impossibly long, all the way to the shore. Murr? And beside it, another shadow cast on the sand . . . I peer closer. The second shadow has no source that I can make out, but if I half-close my eyes, it almost looks like the shape of a woman in a flowing gown, her hand outstretched, as if in blessing or greeting.

Morgelyn, my mum has written in the bottom corner. *Then and always.*

'I thought this was lost,' I hear myself whisper, gripping the frame. 'I thought you'd forgotten.'

When I look up, Davy's expression is strange. He says nothing, only nods to the photograph again. I turn it over and see an envelope, taped to the back of the wood, addressed with only two words.

For Mina

He meets my gaze for a long moment and then, closing his eyes in pain, gestures for me to read.

Sinking onto the bed, I break the seal and draw out the pages.

Dear Mina,

There's one story I never told you.

It begins on a Midsummer Eve, the shortest night of the year, not so very long ago. It begins with a woman who stepped outside a small pub and decided to take an evening stroll around an island, away from the merriment and music, with nothing but the sandy paths and the cries of the curlews to guide her.

Her arms were bare and tanned, her face sun-pinked, her long dress stained with salt from wading through the shallows and as she walked, she sang, an old song from her mother's country, half-remembered.

And all around her the heather bloomed and the gorse gave off its heady scent, so sweet she grew dizzy with it. And as the air turned the colour of mead, she reached the top of the hill and realised she was not alone.

A cat sat there on the headland, proud and silent, its eyes as green as the sea and its fur like shadows. And because the woman had been raised on the old stories — where animals are not always what they seem at the turning of the year — she bowed to the cat, and told it her name, and asked if she might take its photograph with the camera slung over her shoulder.

When the cat blinked once, she took that as a yes and raised the camera to her eye. And what do you know — through the lens she saw there was no cat at all, just a blur of shadow and light, like the first gleam of the sun at

dawn. And before she could press the shutter, the cat
turned and trotted away, down a sandy path towards the
shore, its tail waving like a flag.

And because it was an evening like no other, and because
her head was swimming with cider and scent of the gorse,
she followed it, not knowing what she would find. Of course
she found a tiny cove, where the shore was scattered with
marine wildflowers and a cottage stood, its grey stones soft
in that honeyed light.

She could not help herself, it was so beautiful. She
raised her camera again and took the image. Only when she
lowered it did she see someone step through the door, his
sleeves rolled back and a pencil in his hand. A man with hair
the colour of silver-streaked sand and eyes as changeable
as the sea.

And she stared because, for a moment, she didn't know if
he was real or a trick of the midsummer light. But the cat
looked up from the doorstep where it sat and yowled, as if
to admonish the man for his lack of manners.

'Are you lost?' he called.

Yes, she almost said, but instead she laughed and told him,
no, she was just walking.

And as the cat strolled forwards to bump around her
legs, the man smiled shyly and asked if she would like to take
another photo.

She did want to, and she said so, because the light
was so perfect and so strange. She took image
after image, until she had captured the cottage
with its glinting studio and the shadows among the
heather, and the wild frothing sea lavender and tall,
springing foxgloves and the glittering waves beyond the
secret cove.

All the while, the man sat on the step, talking of this and that and drinking bright wine from a tumbler and playing with the cat, who leaped and pounced at stems of grass.

And the woman remembered herself, and held out a hand and introduced herself as Helena Martinovszky.

The man took her outstretched hand. His own was marked by flecks of paint. 'Davy Penhallow,' he said.

The woman was surprised and asked him whether he was the painter, the one whose work she had seen in the galleries during her course here, the one people called The Old Man of Winter.

The Old Man smiled and told her that he was, and the woman smiled and said he didn't look old at all, and the man explained that the nickname was due to the premature silver in his hair, which he'd had almost since he was a boy.

The two fell to talking, and he fetched a glass and poured out seaberry wine and soon it was as if they had known each other for years. That evening, the light never seemed to fade, and the world was one of sun-warmed stone and bee-stung gorse. The cat, whose name was Murr, sat between them, and when they stroked her soft coat, their hands met and her fur sparked electricity.

The man looked into the woman's eyes, and in that instant he knew she had come carrying the future on the soles of her feet; she had come to change the pattern of all that had gone before. And he wondered if she felt it too, that wondering, that moment no one can explain, when two people see what could be, without a word.

And though her fourth finger bore a gold ring, he asked if she would like to come back the next day, and she said yes. The day after that, when her study group departed the islands for the mainland, she did not go with them. She appeared on the path with a camera around her neck and a canvas bag on her back and asked if she could stay.

And when she held out her hand, the ring was gone, and when he touched her cheek and left a smudge of charcoal there, it was as simple as the seasons between them; it was as if nothing else would ever matter.

Two weeks she stayed with him, in the cottage cut adrift from the world. Days seeped into nights seeped into days; gorse honey and seaberry wine, salt water on skin and hot sand underfoot and a crown of heather on her dark hair, her soft breathing as she drowsed in the shade with the grey cat curled in the crook her arm. There was nothing and no one to break the spell they wove in that endless midsummer until they were as lost as castaways, tangled in each other's souls.

But time cannot be held back, not even by love. And when the summer weather broke, life came welling up around them, washing under the door of the cottage and she knew she had to go. She owed her husband an explanation, she said, but would be back, and so he let her go, with a sprig of dried sea holly and a whispered phrase: yn hav, porth kov gwav. In summer, remember winter.

Every day after that he looked for her, as the summer waned and the wildflowers withered. Letters arrived without her, just another few weeks, she said, things were so difficult. And the man painted in a way he never had before, because nothing else eased the ache he felt at her absence.

Autumn turned to winter and finally, when the old year was almost done, she sent him a photograph of the child within her body, and told him of her and her husband's news and asked if he would be a godfather to her daughter. She said that, though it tore her heart in two, she had been raised to keep the promise she had once made to another man, sealed with a band of gold beneath the eyes of God. The time they had spent together on Morgelyn had been a beautiful dream, but reality had been waiting for her in London, and awful truth that — if she wanted to keep her family — she would have to keep her vow.

And though sorrow raked at him like a storm, he said he understood. He took a rare trip to London for the christening, hoping that he might have been deceived, that their feelings for each other might have withered with the flowers, leaving something gentle and insubstantial in their place. But they had not. She was more beautiful than ever; her cheeks glowing and her arms sheltering that new life, and when she looked at him, there was longing in her gaze, even as her husband took her arm and guided her into the church.

The thorn in the man's chest bit deep, and it was all he could do to sign the register, his ink pen spattering green upon the page. He did not stay long. He fled back to his cottage, to his cat and his cove and he never painted summer again.

The blooming garden was too painful, the smell of gorse flowers and sweet wine too much like her. From then on he worked only when the waves crashed cold, when the light was pale and distant and summer was locked tight beneath the earth where it could not hurt him.

Then, one biting December morning not far from Midwinter's Eve, he looked up to see his cat come trotting along the sandy path, leading a figure. And he was terrified, in case she was a trick of the winter light. But the gorse

whispered and the sand crunched, and it was her, her eyes
bright with cold.

'Hello', she said, as if eight years had not passed.

From behind her, a little face peeped out at him,
with soft brown hair and fierce brown eyes, one of them
streaked with grey like the sea, like the holly, like the
winter. A little girl in a red coat, who reached out to pat the
purring cat.

'This is Mina', the woman told him, a sob half-hitched in her
chest. He told them to come inside, and when he saw that
her finger was bare of a ring, the thorn in his heart sent
out a shoot. Soon they were sat around the fire, drinking
hot chocolate with Murr between them, as it always should
have been.

While the little girl slept, she told him everything: about
the hard years that had followed, about how she had finally
found the courage to leap from the wreckage of her
marriage, and come back to the safe haven she had longed
for across the years. She begged his forgiveness, and —
as the fire smouldered in the grate — he had held her
tight and told her there was nothing to forgive.

That Yuletide — and the weeks that followed — were
a joy, like none he could remember. Two months of blustery
walks and warm spiced hot chocolate, of laughter as Murr
leaped and danced, of the scent of sea holly and the feel
of the woman's fingers twined through his while they slept.
Two months of the little girl's bright chatter, the candlelight
reflected in her wide eyes, the smudges of crayon on her
hands, the way he could look around the door of the room
that was always meant for her every night to see her fast
asleep, one arm wrapped about Murr, who stayed with her,
the guardian of her rest.

And when they lit the candles from the Yule log in the grate, he made a wish that these days could last for ever, and repeated it until the wax guttered into a pool.

But time moves, whether we want it to or not. January went and February came and the sea holly shrivelled above the door and they had to return to the city, so the girl could see the man she called her father, and Helena could unpick the knot of her life there, so that the threads might be gathered up and carried here, for ever.

A few days, she whispered, as they held each other by the path. She would drop her daughter off for a week's visit with her father, then drive straight back.

She kept her word. On a freezing February night she drove towards Cornwall to be with him. But she never reached the islands. A storm, a dark night, a driver who shouldn't have been on the road, bad luck, the wrong place, the wrong time … and she was gone.

You know the rest, dear Mina.

What could I do but mourn her, my heart turned to dust in my chest? What could I do but write to you, and hope you remembered some joy from your time here? What could I do, then, but respect your silence when I got no reply?

I was little more than a kindly stranger to you. You already had a father. You already had a life, far from this place. You already had suffered so much loss. I told myself that I must wait, and that if your heart called you back to Morgelyn, Murr and I would be waiting.

I hope you have come. I hope that I am sitting beside you as you read this; that I live to see another Christmas with you.

But if I do not, then I hope you will be here on the Christmas Eve, dear Mina, as the old year ends and the new begins. If you are, Murr will show you that what we love is never lost; that it is all around us in every flower and thorn, upon every wave and every breath of wind. You are here and so am I. And so is she — then, and always.

> With all my love,
> Your father

'Davy,' I whisper. Tears run down my face, drip onto the bottom of the letter. I look up at the man in the bed, so dear to me, lost for so long. 'Davy, is this true? Are you ...?'

He nods, tears seeping into the deep creases of his cheeks. Heart bursting, I lean down and wrap my arms around him, this man who has changed my life, who loved my mother so briefly and so fiercely, who has given me more than anyone else could.

'I love you, Davy.'

'Love you, Mina,' he cries in return. 'Always ... have.'

CHAPTER NINETEEN

The next day dawns cold, the temperature plummeting. I open the door to find the milk I put out for Murr frozen in its bowl, untouched. A thick frost coats the heather and gorse, melting only reluctantly in the salty air. I call Murr's name again and again into the chilly morning, until my throat is raw and my feet are numb and I have to close the door again with a heavy heart.

The cottage seems strange without Murr; I keep reaching for the pantry door, or for the milk to refill the bowl on the step, or glancing at her cushion beside the fire, only to stop. Even the cove feels empty without her, somehow expectant, as if the sea has breathed out, and won't breathe in again until she gallops across the beach.

Davy too seems sad, even with the barrage of visitors who keep arriving, laden down with gifts and Christmas presents, until finally, I tell them he has to sleep.

Only then do I step outside, switch on my phone and do what I know I must.

My breath mists in the sparkling air as if all the questions inside my heart were taking shape at once. Stomach trembling, I wait for the phone to ring.

It is answered within seconds.

'Mina?' It's my dad's voice, saturated with relief. 'Thank goodness. I've been so worried—'

'I know, Dad.' He must hear something in my tone, because he stops talking at once and doesn't interrupt. 'I know everything, about who Davy is.'

I close my eyes, expecting my father to use his sharp, logical voice, telling me that Davy Penhallow is lying once again, that I'm a fool to believe him. Instead, he makes a noise in the back of his throat, a choke or a cough.

'He told you?'

'Yes. He's awake now. He had a stroke but should recover. We hope.' The sea wind whispers across the cove, stirring the burned bracken, and I think of my mother and how hard it must have been, living in London while her heart lay here. I have to clear my throat in order to force the words out.

'Have you always known?'

There's a long silence. When my father speaks, his voice is shaking. 'In my heart, I did. In my head too, the timings hardly matched up.' He tries for a self-mocking laugh. 'But I told Helena we were man and wife, that this was what we needed to make it work. And then you were born, and we tried to stay together for your sake, far longer than we should have.' His voice breaks. 'If only I'd known what would happen . . .'

'You knew it was Davy?'

'Of course I knew.' There's a mote of bitterness, beneath the sorrow. 'The second I saw him at the christening, the way they looked at each other. It terrified me, Mina. I thought I would lose you both. And so I pressured her to stay, so many times. Until it all fell apart between us. I can't say why she never left before. Only she could tell you that.'

I squeeze my eyes closed, hot tears burning in the cold air. '*You* should have told me.'

'I was too scared.' I can tell he's dredging words from somewhere dark and painful. 'I didn't know what do. Every time I saw you drawing or painting, it made me think of *him*, that he might one day appear to tell the truth and make you hate me. So I tried to keep you safe, tried to keep everything to do with him at a distance, but all I did was push you away.' He is crying now, and my own eyes spill over, salt slicking my face. 'You were right,' he chokes. 'Davy would have done a better job as a father. I'm so sorry, Mina.'

For a long while, I can't speak, just cry with him, my phone pressed to my ear like a shell, filled with the sound of his remorse and sorrow. Finally, I take a deep breath and open my eyes, looking up at blue-gold winter sky.

'Maybe that's true,' I tell him, wiping my nose. 'Maybe it isn't. But you are my father too. Nothing is going to change that.'

'I think part of me suspected,' I tell Jem and Elodie, as we sit by the fire in the Helm, drinking mulled cider on the afternoon of Christmas Eve.

They know everything now, or as much as I do.

When neither of them replies, I look into their guilty expressions. 'You knew?' I ask, incredulous. 'About Davy and my mother?'

'No!' Elodie exclaims. 'I mean, sort of. We wondered.'

'But it wasn't for us to tell,' Jem says, watching my face. 'It was between you and Davy.'

We drink in silence for a while, watching the pearlescent waves through the window. The Helm is safe, at least for now, thanks to the donations that poured in on Midwinter's Eve. Enough to pay the back rent and see them through until the summer, *if* the Penhallows don't force them out.

'What about your dad?' Jem asks. 'Have you heard from him again?'

I nod. On my phone, there's an email that arrived earlier this morning.

> **These were hers.**
>
> **I'm sorry, for everything.**
>
> **All my love,**
>
> **Dad**

And attached to the email, a zip folder containing dozens of photographs. All of them my mother's, from that golden summer she spent with Davy, and more from our few months together on Morgelyn, bright, beautiful images of a time I had thought lost.

'It's going to take some time. But I think we'll be OK,' I tell them.

Elodie nods and drains her drink. 'Better be getting back to the kitchen – Gramps is full-steam ahead with the eight-course festive tasting menu ...' She stops as the noise of a speedboat engine cuts through the air. I recognise it immediately and leap to my feet, rushing to the door in time to see a sleek white vessel pulling up at the jetty.

But it isn't Olivia who climbs the ladder; it's Sam, her blonde hair wild from the sea, wearing an old waterproof jacket.

'What's she doing here?' Jem asks.

Elodie just folds her arms, as Sam walks towards us, her cheeks pink in the freezing air. She doesn't look her usual polished self. There are purple rings beneath her eyes, as if she hasn't slept.

Reaching us, she takes a deep breath. 'I heard that you ... I heard that Davy's back.'

'No thanks to you and your sister.' My voice comes out hard. 'They were keeping him on sedatives, Sam.'

'I didn't know.' Her eyes fill with tears, but she blinks hard, pushing them away. 'I just came to say that I'm sorry for everything. Livvy finally told me last night that the estate's horribly in debt – she's been too afraid to tell anyone about it. That's why she was so desperate to develop. It's no excuse, though.'

'She could have hurt people,' Elodie says. 'She would have left us homeless.'

Sam takes a deep breath. 'I know. And you're right. I should have done more. I've always just . . . let her take charge. I'm sorry for that, truly.' Reaching into her jacket, she takes out a packet of papers. 'Here. I saw the estate solicitor and had this drawn up. Livvy signed it.'

Lips tight, Elodie takes the papers and glances down. It's only a moment before her eyes widen and her mouth falls open.

'What is it?' Jem asks, moving protectively towards his sister.

'It's a new lease for the Helm,' Elodie mutters, still reading. 'Granting it to us in perpetuity for a peppercorn rent of—'

'One jar of potted shrimp per annum,' Sam says, a tiny smile on her face. 'If requested.'

For a long moment, Elodie looks at her, torn between disbelief and joy and hurt. 'No,' she says, thrusting the papers back at Sam. 'I don't want your charity.'

'It isn't charity. It's how things should be. This place is your family's home, yours and your grandfather's. You should never have to be afraid of losing it.'

When Elodie doesn't answer, Sam reaches into her coat for another envelope. 'The offer's there, anyway. And Mina . . . this is for you. I'm sorry again for everything.' She casts one last look at Elodie. 'Merry Christmas, El.'

As she walks away, I rip open the envelope to find the power of attorney form, and there at the bottom, in green ink, Davy's forged signature.

'It's safe,' I tell them both, disbelief rushing through me. 'Davy's cottage is safe.'

'So is the Helm,' Jem says, still reading the papers.

Elodie doesn't answer, staring after Sam.

'Come on,' Jem nudges her. 'Let's go tell Gramps.'

Gryff, as it turns out, shares none of Elodie's reservations. He breaks into song when he sees the papers and parades around the kitchen using his ladle as a baton, before insisting on opening a bottle of champagne.

It's with a light head, and the feel of Jem's hands on my cheeks as he said goodbye that I stagger over to the village shop. It's busy, the windows fogged up with breath, the radio blaring out festive songs. Half the island is crammed between the shelves, drinking port and sherry and eating mince pies. A cheer goes up when I enter and, for a few minutes, I find myself laughing among them, answering questions about Davy, about our Christmas plans.

'Just a quiet one, I think,' I yell over the blaring of the music.

'Have you a crab?' Kevin asks seriously. 'Here, I'll fetch you one . . .'

'And you must take some sloe gin,' one of the old ladies presses. 'Davy loves a bit of gin.'

Eventually, I make it out, my face hot, arms groaning beneath the bags of food and drink and fresh crab and biscuits and cake pressed onto me.

'Mina!' a voice calls. It's Gryff, his eyes still bright. He stuffs a jar of potted shrimp into my coat pocket. 'Just in case,' he says sadly.

I arrive back at the cottage just as the district nurse is leaving. 'His pulse isn't very strong,' she tells me quietly, packing away her bag. 'But he insists he feels all right. Just tired.'

I glance into the bedroom where Davy lies, his hands folded on the blanket.

'What can I do?'

She gives me a sad smile as she pulls on her coat. 'Nothing. It's up to him now. Just be here, keep him company.'

When I look in on Davy a few minutes later, he's struggling to get out of bed.

'What are you doing?' I scold. 'You have to rest.'

'Christmas . . . Eve,' he says. His voice is slow and laboured, but when he looks at me, his eyes are bright. 'Work to do.'

As dusk falls, Davy sends me out onto the cove to collect sprigs of sea holly and wild thyme, heather and gorse from the undamaged parts of the thicket. The wind is biting, chilling my hands and face, the clouds thick and pale purple and, for a moment, I'm convinced I smell snow. Back inside, Davy shows me with clumsy gestures how to bind the greenery together into a wreath.

'Like the one from your story,' I say, and he gives me a crooked smile.

I use the rest of the foliage to decorate the cottage, hanging boughs above the ship-wreck mantel, a fresh sprig above the door to ward off bad spirits, laying gorse upon the windowsills, where it catches the light of the oil lanterns and glows like gold. Soon the cottage fills with the scent of salt and fresh-cut greenery and the delicate fragrance of winter flowers.

From the wardrobe, he has me pull out an old sea chest. Inside, carefully wrapped in newspaper, are decorations from across the centuries. Some look ancient, carved from bone or driftwood. A painful word at a time, Davy tells me their stories: a metal sun that is four hundred years old, brought here by a Dutch sailor. A leaping cat carved by his great-grandfather as he rode the winter waves. And the oldest of them, a woman shaped out of stone, or a stone that happens to be shaped like a woman, flecks of mica sparking in the rock like frost or glittering salt.

I place them around us, nestle them among the gorse branches and hang them from the lantern bracket and the cottage's exposed beams, until they sway and glint like stars, the treasured flotsam of centuries.

Davy smiles, pointing to the last decoration in the box. 'My favourite.'

Slowly, I pull out a blue felt fish. The one I made so many years ago, the one I wanted to give to Murr on Christmas Day.

Heart aching, I meet his eyes. His face looks older than ever, yet there's a light in his gaze that makes him seem youthful.

'Did . . . ever tell you, Mina?' he says, careful with every word.

I shake my head, recognising this as the start of one of his stories. When Davy gestures towards the bookcase, I understand at once, and slowly run my finger over the spines, stopping when he nods vigorously.

I pull the book out. It's a thin, leather-bound volume, published by a small press. '*Stories for Midwinter* by Davy Penhallow,' I read with a smile.

Kneeling beside his chair, I help him turn the pages until we reach the introduction. With a trembling hand, he motions for me to read.

With a glance at him, I clear my throat. '"People have always told tales on the night between Christmas Eve and Christmas Day in the morning, to entertain those whose heads are full of honey and amuse those whose bellies are full of warmth. But what people are really doing, when they tell those tales, is weaving the old magic."' Despite the heat of the fire, a shiver goes through me. '"Because Christmas Eve is the one night of the year when the animals can speak, and the rocks can sing and the sea itself can whisper to us, if only we learn how to listen . . ."'

CHAPTER TWENTY

As I read, the words on the page seem to sway and shift like smoke. Or is it the cottage around me? From the corner of my eye, I see the candles on the windowsill flutter in a breeze I cannot feel. The leaping cat twists, as if jumping over the waves. The stone woman sparks in the firelight. And I remember the strange song that I dreamed, on my first night here; I remember the green fire in Murr's gaze as she looked at me, the way her shadow seemed to fill the whole cottage. I look up to see that Davy's eyes are closed.

The people who went before are all around us, Mina, if only we could learn to hear them . . .

I close my eyes, and listen.

At first I hear nothing, just the crack and pop of the flames in the grate, just the quiet hush of the waves on the beach. But then there is something, at the limit of my hearing; as loud as the far-off roar of the Atlantic, as quiet as the drone of a bee in a gorse flower, as gentle as a rumbling purr.

I open my eyes and Davy is gone; in the chair instead sits a woman, hair black as a guillemot's wing, a little boy with silver-streaked hair sleeping on the hearthrug at her feet, his arms wrapped around a large grey cat for comfort, now that his father will never come home again. In the space between one blink and another the woman becomes a little girl, chasing a grey cat through a cottage crowded with people, filled to the beams with laughter and song and red cheeks, the smell of stolen spices and smuggled brandy as the islanders spill out onto the dark beach to wassail the sea and ask for a good year.

I drift along with them, caught up in the merriment until, in a blink, they vanish. A young man in the clothes of another time stands alone on the sandy path, clutching a seabag, coming home after so long. His tanned face creases with joy at the sight of the cottage as a grey cat trots out to meet him. I take a step towards them only to stumble and fall to my knees. There on the sand, a young woman in a sodden shift kneels, thumping a man's chest as he splutters out seawater, as a creature with sea-green eyes watches on.

Movement flickers at the corner of my eye and I turn to see a young woman walk down towards the shore. Her hair is lank and she wears roughly woven clothes, a worn sheepskin, but she carries something in her hands: a wreath of sea holly, which she casts onto the waves, in thanks. A creature pads beside her, its smoke-grey fur matted.

Murr! I open my mouth to call out only to be engulfed by a vast, icy wave. Surfacing with a gasp, coughing out brine, I hear a yowl and look up to see Murr perched on an outcrop, her fur as wet as weeds. Just as another wave towers above me, I push myself upwards and scramble onto the safety of the rock, beside the cat who hisses and spits at the storm, sparking electricity.

I swipe at my eyes only to realise that there's no saltwater, no pummelling waves. I'm lying on the cold sand of the cove, in the shadow of the burned furze, alone. Frightened, head spinning, I push myself to my knees only to see something glimmer through the charred branches. Hesitantly, I crawl forwards and reach out to touch grey stone, smooth as glass. Whatever it is, it's half-buried in the earth and I scrabble at it, sandy soil catching my nails, burned bracken crushing beneath my knees as I scrape until it finally comes free.

The moment it's in my hands, I know what it is. The stone is made from the same substance as the figurine on Davy's mantel, glimmering with mica that shines like frost or salt or starlight. But where that one is shaped like a woman, this one is shaped like a cat; a grey cat, with a round body, one paw upraised. It looks old; so old that the marks of carving are lost to time, if human hands ever carved this at all.

'Murr,' I whisper. In response, the endless song of the sea and the land floods my mind. And in a flash, I finally understand what Davy's stories were trying to tell me. That with every step we take, we change the land and are changed by it in turn. The land remembers us, just as we must remember.

She is here, then and always.

Light sparkles through the tears that hang on my eyelashes, and I look up just as the sun crests the sea, turning everything golden, spreading dawn on the first day of the new year's turning.

And, standing among those bright waves, I think I see someone: a woman smiling at me, holding out a hand, in a blessing.

Yma hi orth diwedhva an vledhen goth ha dallethva an vledhen nowydh. At the old year's ending and the new year's beginning . . .

A noise jolts me awake. I'm slumped on the hearth rug, my legs numb, the fire burned down to embers. Beside me, Davy sleeps in the armchair, snoring softly. When I push myself up, his book of stories tumbles to the floor. I must have fallen asleep reading them. But then why are my hands blackened with soot? Why can I taste seawater at the back of my throat?

Then the noise comes again, quietly at first, but growing louder: the clanking of a stone bowl, a soft sound that could be a mew. Heart racing, I lurch to my feet and throw open the door.

White, that's what I see first, and for a moment I stare bewildered until I realise that it's snow. A fine layer coats the sand, glittering in the pale golden light of dawn. Blinking, not wanting to believe, I look down.

A cat sits on the step, fur as soft and grey as smoke, poking at the frozen milk in the bowl, and licking at her paw. A set of paw prints lead out from the burned furze, where a grey stone glimmers in the shadows. Looking up at me with sea-green eyes, she lets out an indignant meow.

'Murr!'

With a sob of joy, I scoop her into my arms and bury my face in her soft fur. She smells of snow and salt, heather and gorse and new, green shoots.

'Mina?' Davy asks, and I turn to see him leaning from his chair, face twisted with hope. When he sees Murr, he lets out a cry of happiness.

I drop Murr onto his lap and she kneads the blanket madly, rubbing her face all over his chin until her purring and our laughter fill the cottage, louder even than the sea.

EPILOGUE

One Christmas Later

'Oi, you rabble!' Elodie yells. 'I'm trying to read.'

I smile over at her. Her face is flushed from food and wine and laughter, paper hat askew on her dark hair. Ten of us are crammed around Davy's kitchen table, the remains of Gryff's five-course dinner in front of us, complete with Christmas crab. Leticia looks more than a little tipsy, her hat sliding off, Jem is laughing at something with Paola, while Davy and Mo talk animatedly about some local legend.

'Quiet!' Sam laughs, her blonde hair perfectly swept up, catching the light. Beside the fire Philip snoozes, full of sausages, wearing a red and white striped coat.

'Thank you, dear.' Elodie flaps yesterday's edition of the paper. 'Right.'

'Anyone for trifle?' Gryff breaks in. 'My own recipe. No fish included.'

'Gramps!'

'Sorry, sorry.'

Elodie clears her throat. 'Last week, a cove on the island of Morgelyn was granted protected status after a year-long campaign by residents to officially recognise it as a site of historical importance.'

A cheer goes around the table, people clinking glasses, before Elodie raises her voice again.

'A sixth-century votive statue, carved to represent a cat, and now named the Murr Stone, was discovered last December by Morgelyn-based illustrator, Mina Kestle, whose own work has recently been displayed in St Martin's Gallery ...'

Another cheer goes around the table, and I can't help but laugh. Davy squeezes my arm, just as he did back in the summer, when I stood, sick with nerves, on the opening night of my first exhibition.

'The discovery of the statue has provoked much interest from national and international historical groups,' Elodie ploughs on. 'And after discussions with experts and island residents, it was decided that the Murr Stone will remain in situ, covered by a bespoke shelter—'

'I'll have it done after we get back from London, I promise,' Jem laughs.

'... and that its preservation will be overseen by local archivist and historian, Mo Said, who will also be in charge of a satellite museum site.'

Mo raises his hands to the round of applause, smiling bashfully until Elodie clears her throat with purpose.

'Mina Kestle, the daughter of well-known local artist and writer Davy Penhallow, commented: "I can't take any credit for discovering the Stone. Its exact location might have been forgotten, but the story of Morgelyn and her cat has always been remembered, in tale and song, by those who know and love this place."'

'Hear, hear,' Davy says, raising his glass.

Another round of toasts goes ahead, Paola popping the cork and filling glasses, the table making swift work of my father's gift of a crate of champagne.

'And where is herself?' Davy asks. 'She isn't even here to enjoy her fame.' He peers over at the armchair, where Murr sprawls in a fluffy heap, belly full of potted shrimp and crab. 'Get up, you lazy beast.'

Murr opens an eye and gives a giant yawn as if to say, *I am not to be disturbed.* With a laugh, Davy heaves himself from the chair and gathers Murr up with his good arm, placing her on my lap.

'To my girls,' he says, raising a glass.

'To family,' Gryff adds, misty-eyed.

'To Christmas,' toasts Paola.

'To new friends.' Lou clinks glasses with her.

'And old,' Leticia says.

'To change,' Sam says softly.

'To love,' Elodie answers.

'To the past,' Mo says.

Jem reaches for my free hand, where a ring with a stone of green sea glass glimmers. 'To the future.'

'To the new year and the old,' I say, and look down at the cat on my lap. Murr gazes back, her green eyes bright. 'To the one who brought us all together here, then, and always.' I stroke her head. 'To Murr.'

'To Murr!' the cry goes up, laughter and merriment ringing from the walls of the little cottage.

And outside, just for a moment among the new-budding gorse, a woman seems to turn and smile, before vanishing in a flurry of snow on the sea wind.

ACKNOWLEDGEMENTS

From the first word on a page to the final checks, there are so many people who come together to make a book a reality. So, to everyone who has worked on *A Midwinter's Tail* – from editing, production, translation, distribution, bookselling – thank you.

Anne; I can confidently say this book wouldn't exist without you! Thanks also to Meg at Ki, to Hélène, to my brilliant editor Bec and the whole team at Sphere. Special thanks to Nazia, fellow cat-lover and publicist extraordinaire.

Thanks go to my crew of friends, not least Emma, for always being there on the other end of a phone screen. Thank you to my family: to C&D for the support, Dad for the stories, Mum for your unwavering faith, and – always – Lucy. Grammie, I wish you could have read this.

Nick, thanks for everything you do to lift me up (including sending me cat videos when I'm down). And lastly, thank you to the feline companions I've known over the years, for bringing joy in so many ways.

ABOUT THE AUTHOR

Lili Hayward is the author of *A Midwinter's Tail* and *The Cat of Yule Cottage*. As Laura Madeleine she also writes bestselling historical fiction, which has been translated into over a dozen languages. She lives with her partner in Bristol, UK.

Want more?
To read a free festive short story visit
lauramadeleine.com/midwinter